I0681245

Debt Slave

MINDING HIS MASTER

SAMANTHA CAYTO

ENTWINED PUBLISHING

Minding his Master
ISBN # 978-1-80250-715-7
©Copyright Samantha Cayto 2025
Cover Art by Kelly Martin ©Copyright January 2025
Interior text design by Entwined Publishing
Published by Entice, an Entwined Publishing imprint

This is a work of fiction. All characters, places and events are from the author's imagination and should not be confused with fact. Any resemblance to persons, living or dead, events or places is purely coincidental.

All rights reserved. No part of this book may be used, reproduced, or distributed in any form or by any means, including but not limited to electronic, mechanical, photocopying, recording, or by any information storage and retrieval system, without prior written permission from the publisher. This book and its contents are expressly reserved from use in training artificial intelligence technologies or systems. Furthermore, this work is expressly reserved from the text and data mining exception, in accordance with Directive (EU) 2019/790 of the European Parliament and of the Council.

Applications should be addressed in the first instance, in writing, to Entwined Publishing. Unauthorised or restricted acts in relation to this publication may result in civil proceedings and/or criminal prosecution.

The author and illustrator have asserted their respective rights under the Copyright Designs and Patents Acts 1988 (as amended) to be identified as the author of this book and illustrator of the artwork.

Published in 2025 by Entwined Publishing, United Kingdom.

Entwined Publishing is a division of Totally Entwined Group Limited.

MINDING HIS MASTER

Chapter One

Tate stared down the pristine triple black diamond trail, savoring the adrenaline rush that he always felt before starting a challenge to his skills and mortality. The resort had advertised this run as the ultimate skiing experience, for experts only. Now, as he scanned what he could see through the trees, taking in the near vertical slope, large moguls and even cliffs in the distance, he was delighted to see first-hand that the trail was as advertised. Only the best and even craziest skiers would risk a run like this. And because people meeting that description were few and far between, he had it all to himself. *Perfect.* Whether he was racing cars, surfing monster waves, free solo climbing, base jumping, or any other extreme sport, he preferred to be on his own, allowing his adrenal gland to do its thing in private. And when he reached the bottom, he'd feel — just for a little while — what it was like to be alive and happy again.

He closed his eyes for a few seconds, inhaling the scents of the woods and listening to the hearty bits of nature that stirred in the bitter cold, then launched himself down the trail.

The run started out perfectly. His surroundings blurred as he sped past the first stand of trees. The cold air slapped at what little of his face was bare. It was almost too easy for him to maneuver his way. His body knew what to do, how to twist with the turns. His skis were extensions of his feet and his poles of his hands. He let his instincts control his movements while his brain enjoyed the sensation of flying down the mountain side. The first mogul he hit was a piece of cake, and he laughed out loud as he briefly left the ground. He absorbed the impact on landing as if his legs were made of springs. Looking ahead, he spied the cliff coming up and his heart rate kicked up to an eleven. He didn't even try to slow before taking it.

For a few glorious seconds, he sailed through the air, unfettered and no longer weighed down by the heaviness of being Tate Graham, scion to two of the wealthiest families in the world, not the chosen son but now the *only* son, destined to take the reins of the two conglomerates that would one day pass into his hands. However unwilling he was to take them. No, as he flew toward the slope, he was simply himself, with no one there to press upon him his heavy responsibilities.

The moment he landed on the untouched powdery snow, he knew he'd made a mistake. He'd miscalculated by some fraction where and how his body should be. He didn't panic—he never did. Instead, he corrected his stance and steered himself in the right direction. Except it didn't work. Rare as it was, his instincts in controlling his body and his environment were off, just a bit, which was enough. He couldn't get himself heading back on the trail again. A large tree loomed in front of him.

Tate made one last effort in the milliseconds he had to avoid disaster. He failed, and ran head on into the unyielding bark.

* * * *

"The only surprising thing is that this hasn't happened before now."

Tate opened his eyes to narrow slits at the sound of his mother's voice. Her tone dripped with disgust more than worry. In the dim light of his hospital room, he saw his parents standing at the end of his bed. Their body language screamed impatience, outrage and exasperation.

His father put his hand on his mother's shoulder. "Think of it this way, Liz, at least he'll be incapacitated for a while and won't be able to take any more risks. This isn't an injury he can simply shake off."

His mother grimaced before saying, "There is that, I suppose. Silver linings and whatnot."

Tate wasn't bothered by their lack of sympathy or worry that their son was... He took stock of how he'd been hurt. The skiing accident was fresh in his mind, so he wasn't confused about why he was lying in a hospital. But for his parents to have been summoned and to actually have come to his bedside, it had to be bad. His head ached dully, muted by the fuzziness of painkillers. His right arm was in a sling, as was his right leg. Enough discomfort broke through the meds for him to understand he'd broken something in each location. His mouth was as dry as it had been during that car race across the Sahara, which made him think he might have had surgery.

He must have made some kind of noise because good old Mom and Dad turned in unison, frowning. It would have been comical if their demeanor didn't make him want to cry, throw up and scream in any and all orders. God, he was so sick of their judgment and disapproval. If he could have sat up and left, he would. But he was weak as a kitten and not a little disoriented.

His mother did all the talking, as usual. "You're awake, finally. Thank God for that. The doctor said your concussion was severe but at least you didn't fracture your skull."

Tate forced a word past his dry lips. "Helmet."

"Yes, well, you've always been a safety-first kind of boy." She walked to the side of his bed near his head and picked up a cup on the nightstand. She held the straw to his lips so that he could drink some of the tepid water inside.

When he pulled away, his mother set it back down and glared at him. "Do you want a catalog of your various injuries?"

Not really.

It was a rhetorical question. "In addition to the concussion, you broke your collarbone and right femur." She leaned a little closer to him. "There was bone sticking out of your leg when they cut off your ski pants." The way she relayed that information, there was a certain amount of relish with a subtext of *this is no more than you deserved.* "And somehow, despite the injuries being mainly on your right side, you also ruptured your spleen. Congratulations, Tate, you've managed to scare your father and me half to death. It's been just like…" She turned and shook her head.

Now Tate really felt like crap. His parents were nearly psychopathic in nature, but every once in a while, they showed slivers of real caring, and he did feel shitty about scaring them into thinking they were going to lose another son.

"Sorry," he managed to rasp out. Of course that one show of weakness gave them the opening they wanted.

His mother turned to him again, the look in her eyes warning him he wasn't going to like what she was about to say. "As soon as the doctors clear you to leave, we're taking you to Fils-Aime for recovery. It's going to be months before you fully heal."

Tate struggled to sit up, failing. "No. Mom, I don't need to go to the island. I'll go home and hire a nurse, or whatever, to help." Yeah, because with his right arm out of condition, he wasn't going to be able to even wipe his own ass. *Christ.*

Both his parents were shaking their heads before he'd even finished his last sentence. And now his father added his voice to the decision. "Your townhouse isn't big enough for the hospital bed and all of the other things you'll need to recuperate. The island affords a lot more room and is already fully staffed." The man tried for a reassuring smile. "We'll get you a nurse and you can spend time out in the sunny fresh air. It's the perfect place to recuperate. Your mother and I won't be staying, of course."

And wasn't that just the saddest part of this whole damn thing—his parents knew that their not being with him would be a selling point. Still, the idea of being isolated, at the mercy of caretakers on their private island set a wave of near panic over him. He needed to be in control of himself, even though so much in his life was beyond it.

"It's really not necessary." As he once more tried to lift his head, he scanned for his phone and found none of his stuff within reach. Fuck, they had made sure he was completely dependent on them. "I'll be fine at home." Where he would have his phone and could use his friends and his own servants as a shield against his parents until he recovered.

"It's all been decided, Tate." His mother's tone and expression told him he was wasting his breath. Liz and Cliff Graham ruled their domain with ruthless determination. They had the money and the means to bully the hospital staff and even the police if they wanted to.

He was helpless—for the time being. Shutting his eyes, he said, "Fine." This was a temporary imprisonment. With time and effort, he'd be back on his feet and back in command of his own self. He just had to be patient.

* * * *

Caden stood as still as he could, trying not to cringe at the scrutiny of his naked body. The couple sat judging his physical worthiness with the same intensity he imagined they employed with all their acquisitions. From what he could see of their opulent home, they had excellent taste. He couldn't fault the situation he'd landed in. While he'd once been rich, the Grahams were *wealthy*. Whatever else his next ten years were going to be like, at least he'd be living in luxury. And his new master was of an age that he preferred, fit and handsome in the typical country-club way of men like him. It shouldn't be hard to spend time in the man's bed, even though he suspected the wife would at least be watching, if not participating. That was okay. He had no interest in sex with women, but with the husband as a source of arousal, he should manage to get the job done.

"Turn around." It was his mistress who ran the show. That was obvious. Her shrewd gaze took in every bit of him.

Caden proudly showed them his butt, which is what he assumed they were interested in. Asshole Andrew had loved that part of him, always fondling it and even biting it before fucking him blind. The guy had been hung and horny, and that was what had brought Caden's downfall. He'd been kept in a constant state of pleasure and had been ignorant of everything else.

"Hmm," the master murmured. "He's a bit short and skinny. But I don't suppose any of that matters if he knows how to use his mouth and has a tight ass."

"Really, Cliff. Don't be so vulgar. I don't need to know the details of his appeal. We just have to decide if he's right for Tate in the short term."

Tate? Who the hell is Tate? Something tickled the back of his brain. He'd heard of a Tate Graham, hadn't he?

"Right enough," the master said. "He was the best we could get on such short notice, and God knows he's expensive enough. He must be brainless to have gotten himself in such deep debt at his age."

Caden took the criticism without flinching. Mr. Graham was right, after all. Caden had been naïve to the point of imbecility to have missed what Andrew had been doing.

The mistress sighed. "Very well. Get dressed."

It took Caden a few seconds to realize she was giving him an order. He slowly turned to the table where he'd folded his clothes and gasped at the sting of a slap. Blinking at his mistress with shock, he tried to stutter out an apology without really understanding what he'd done wrong.

Mrs. Graham narrowed her gaze. "When you're given an order, you snap to it. Do you understand?"

Caden nodded. "Yes, ma'am. I'm sorry, ma'am." He forced back the tears that threatened to leak out. It was clear now that his life really was in tatters. As a debt slave, he not only had to do what he was told without question, he had to take any abuse meted out. Whatever guardrails the law imposed on such conduct, he wasn't so foolish to believe they were followed. The Grahams could do whatever they liked, knowing that they would never be held to account for their actions.

His mistress left the room with a dismissive toss of her head.

The master came over just as Caden was buttoning up his shirt. The man brushed against him, grabbing Caden's dick with one hand and squeezing his ass with the other. "I'd like to have you myself, but my wife would never tolerate that." He pulled and squeezed hard enough to make Caden wince. "You're a present for our son. He's been badly injured. It's your job to take care of him in all ways. You'll play both nursemaid and whore, keeping him happy and reporting back to us about how entertained he is by you. If you don't do your job well, I'll pass you off to a friend of mine who'd love to have a pretty boy like you in his bed." Graham leaned in closer to whisper against Caden's ear, "You won't like being there, though. I can promise you that." His master released him and walked away. "Finish getting dressed and go out front. My assistant will take you to Tate. I doubt you'll like my son much, either," he added as a parting shot.

Feeling scared and sorrier for himself than he had since his world had fallen apart, Caden hurried to obey.

* * * *

14

Caden was glad the agency had taught him to keep his gaze down. The last thing he wanted was to have to stare into the smug eyes of Mr. Graham's personal assistant, Richard. *Mr. Harding, to you.* As if Caden had popped out with a "hi, Dick" the moment the man had appeared by his side and led him to first a car, and then a private plane. The guy had had a hungry look from the start and had ordered Caden to strip and kneel on one of the seats in order to jerk off to the sight of Caden's hole. It had been humiliating, but at least he hadn't been forced to blow the guy, or worse. No doubt old Dicky was scared shitless of soiling his employer's new slave.

As the plane descended, he dared to look out of the window. Vivid blue-green ocean spread out below them and in the distance, he could see a slice of paradise looming that had to be the private island they were headed to. This would be his home for the next few months as he tended to the Grahams' son. Harding had given him a thorough lecture on the situation. Tate was an extreme sport junky who had pressed his luck too far. A spoiled brat. Only someone with such inherited wealth could afford to spend the kind of time, money and effort to do things that could kill him. Some people risked their lives every day to put food on the table. This guy did it because he was bored. It was that simple, and the idea of it disgusted Caden. And if part of that reaction was a condemnation of how he'd frittered his own short adult life away because he'd had money to burn, well it was no more than he deserved. He would literally slave away in service to this entitled jerk and had no right to complain.

An older black woman dressed in a white shirt and slacks greeted them on the runway once they had deplaned. She gave them a welcoming smile and introduced herself directly to Caden as Miss Ophelia. She even held out her hand for a shake. Caught by surprise, he gave her one, at once embarrassed and grateful for being treated like a human being for the first time in days. No matter how irritating it might be to serve the Graham scion, this woman could prove to be a port in that coming shit storm. And she had balls.

"That you, Mr. Harding," Miss Ophelia said in a lilt born on one of the Caribbean islands. "I'll take him to Mr. Caden and get him settled in. You'll want to take off right away." She glanced at the clear, blue sky. "A storm's coming, they say."

With that, she gently cupped Caden by the arm and led him over to a golf cart-type conveyance. She got behind the wheel and with a lurch, they left down a narrow, paved road and headed toward the rambling, white stucco house he'd seen from the air. It was as huge as it had appeared, and as they went around the back of the building, he spotted a massive pool and what looked like a golf course. *Of course, the Grahams can afford to have whatever they want.* That included a living sex toy whose job was essentially to keep their son pacified in what he figured was a gilded cage.

Miss Ophelia stopped in front of a door and hopped out. Caden understood to follow her without being told. They entered into what was a giant mudroom that led to a restaurant-sized kitchen, gleaming with shiny appliances, and where other staff bustled around. He got the side-eye from each of them as he passed but no one said anything.

"I'm the housekeeper," Miss Ophelia said over her shoulder. "I command the rest of the staff." She jogged up a set of plain stairs, her fitness obvious. "Not you, though. Only Mr. Tate gets to order you around."

No, his parents do that. Caden didn't say that, naturally. He wasn't going to put the woman in an uncomfortable position by spitting out the truth. He needed a friend on this isolated island and the head servant was perfect for that role.

Down the hall they went when they reached the next floor. Miss Ophelia stopped by a closed door. "These are Mr. Tate's rooms."

Rooms. Sure, a guy like Tate would have a suite even in a vacation home.

Caden followed the housekeeper into a sitting room that had floor-to-ceiling windows on one wall with a dazzling view of the ocean. He was mesmerized by the sight so it took him a second to hear the voices coming from the room beyond.

"Really, Mr. Graham. I'm a nurse who has had to wipe more backsides than I can count. Doing it for you doesn't bother me."

"Yeah? Well, here's the thing, Nurse Ratched, it bothers *me*. So let's just get off this endless merry-go-round of an argument each time I need a bedpan and let me do this one little thing for myself. Okay?"

The harried nurse—and boy, didn't Caden feel bad for the woman, and himself given that this was his new job—didn't have a chance to respond. Miss Ophelia strode right into both the bedroom and the disagreement, despite the fact that they were certainly entering at a delicate time.

But, no, actually. The nurse was walking away into a bathroom on the other side, cradling a bed pan, and Tate Graham lay in his hospital bed, lap covered and awkwardly running some kind of wipe through the fingers of his free hand. He wadded the thing up and threw it over the side of the bed as he eyed them. Eyed Caden, really. He shot the housekeeper a brief smile before staring hard at his new slave and the look on his face wasn't welcoming at all.

"Seriously? They really went ahead and did it?" The next few words out of Tate's mouth were sailor-worthy.

Miss Ophelia put her hands on her hips. "I know you're in pain, Mr. Tate, and frustrated by your injuries, but I will remind you to watch your language."

The guy actually looked chastised. "Sorry, Miss Ophelia."

Wow, the lofty Mr. Graham is being very respectful to a servant.

His gaze narrowed as he looked Caden up and down. "It looks like they plucked him out of a skate park, so I have to assume he's not a nurse."

Caden was shaking his head as the actual nurse returned.

"He certainly isn't." Disgust laced the woman's tone. "That's still my job. His is to keep you company and…wipe your ass." The nurse, who according to her name tag was Ms. Schmidt, left the room in a huff.

"I don't want him." Tate spat out that pronouncement as he tried to reposition the pillows behind him. With one arm immobilized and a leg in a sling, he was having a hard time of it.

"Now, Mr. Tate. You know there's no choice in this." Miss Ophelia used the kind of tone one used with a toddler on the brink of a tantrum.

"Like hell. It's bad enough that I've been kidnapped and held against my will. I'll be damned if I'm going to be pacified and distracted by some…pretty…sex…slave. Argh!" He flopped back in defeat against a pile of pillows in complete disarray. They'd only been slightly so before he'd tried to rearrange them.

Fed up with the guy's bitching about something neither of them could control, Caden marched over to the bed. "Here, let me do that. Master," he tacked on because he needed to remember his pitiful place in this world now.

Tate surprised him by sitting up enough to give him room. "Do *not* call me that."

Caden fluffed and lined up the silk-covered pillows to permit Tate to lie back in a more comfortable sitting position. He flicked his gaze at Tate. "Sorry. Sir."

"Not that, either. Christ!" Tate flopped back as soon as Caden stepped away.

Caden took a deep breath and let it out slowly to curb his growing frustration. He stared at the floor, as well, to hide his feelings. "I'm sorry. I'm new to this. What should I call you?"

"*Tate*." His master said his name as if the answer were obvious and it was Caden who was being difficult. He sighed noisily. "Thanks, Miss Ophelia. Sorry for the hissy fit."

"You don't have to apologize to *me*." The woman shook her head before turning on her heel and leaving the room.

Long, awkward seconds ticked by, punctuated by Tate squirming and sighing, as if he couldn't get comfortable no matter his position. Maybe it was pain. Or maybe it was the difficulty of a very active man having to lie about in bed, more of his body contained in medical equipment than not. Caden started to feel sorry for the guy.

Then Tate killed that moment of sympathy by huffing. "What the hell am I supposed to do with you?"

Chapter Two

Tate stared with mounting frustration at his parents' latest manipulation. So, he didn't like being isolated from his friends on this island? No problem. Mom and Dad had the perfect solution. They'd bought him a sex slave to keep him occupied. Not that they had called this kid standing awkwardly by his bedside that exactly. *Personal slave.* That had been the euphemism. *He'll be good company for you.* And by 'good company' his father had really meant hand jobs, and blow jobs and someone who could ride his dick when he felt up to something more strenuous. And this slave would be able to bring him the quarterly financials and other corporate information that they wanted him to study, as if being force-fed that stuff would somehow make him more interested in the family businesses. As if he'd forget that they were only doing this because they had to, that he was their second choice for the role of son and heir.

A shock of pain up his leg made him grimace. He could be more doped-up, but preferred the clarity of mind that came from lower doses of pain meds. The last time he'd allowed himself to be knocked out completely, he'd ended up here—trapped and with no way to contact anyone in the outside world. Everyone on this island worked for his parents and did exactly what they told them. Even Miss Ophelia, who had always been kind to him, was never going to go against their wishes and help him escape. And it would be weeks before he could leave his bed and move around on his own. He was beyond angry.

There was only one person he could take his fury out on.

Tate glared at his slave. "Okay, Nurse Nancy, let's see what Mommy and Daddy bought for me." When the boy looked at him with furrowed brows, Tate clarified. "Take off your clothes."

The boy's Adam's apple bobbed up and down on a hard swallow. "Yes..." He shook his head and complied.

Off came the button-down shirt, then the loafers and socks, and the pants. The boy neatly folded and placed everything on a nearby chair. When he turned to do so, he flashed Tate with a perfectly high, tight ass because the guy was wearing a black thong. The two mounds of pale flesh made his mouth water, and despite his anger and pain, Tate's dick rallied at the sight. The reaction pissed him off even more. He wasn't going to be so easily seduced by his parents' scheme. He needed to hold firm against the temptation thrown at him, or he was going to end up right where they wanted—heeling to their control.

The slave hooked his thumbs on the band of the underwear to shove it down.

"Not that." Tate didn't need the extra provocation of seeing the boy's cock. Besides, he liked the almost-naked look. *God damn it!*

As the boy stood with his gaze cast downward and arms hanging loosely by his side, Tate studied him closely. There was no choice but to do so given how he'd been the one to send them both down this path. The slave was young — barely out of high school by the look of him — and beautiful with streaky blond hair that flopped over his forehead and hung just above bright green eyes. The kind of bed partner he would seek out if he were in a club. His parents had known him well-enough to get that right. It was beyond creepy, and he had no doubt this kid was some kind of spy as well as sex slave. This was a way for them to keep tabs on him twenty-four seven. But there was more to this guy than they probably had noticed. Whoever he was, however he'd landed in such terrible debt that selling himself like this was the only way out, he hated being here. Maybe as much as Tate hated having him. He could see it in flashes of his eyes and the tone of his voice.

Great. An angry master and an angry slave. Wasn't this going to be a fun few months?

"What's your name?"

"Caden."

"Caden what?"

The guy blinked at him a few times before answering. "Graham."

Now it was Tate's turn to blink. His brain short-circuited in an effort to understand. "Holy fuck! Are you saying they sent me some distant relative or something?"

Caden furrowed his brows and looked at Tate as if he'd had a stroke or something. "Um, no." He spoke slowly. "Now that I'm a slave, I take whatever my owner's last name is."

Tate was stunned into silence by the news. Although he was disgusted by the debt slave laws, he hadn't bothered to learn much about them. He certainly had no intention of taking advantage of them himself. His parents, not surprisingly, had no qualms about it. Caden wasn't the first human being they'd bought.

He licked his lips, which were always dry these days. It was because of his injuries, not the provocative sight of a nearly naked guy in front of him.

"Okay. That's moronic, but okay. Let me put it this way, what's the name on your driver's license?"

Caden shifted his feet, darted his gaze around the room before settling back to looking in the vicinity of Tate's chin. "I don't have one. It was canceled along with my passport when I signed the contract." He shrugged. "They don't want me running away instead of terminating the agreement and incurring a break-up fee along with reacquiring the debt."

Tate was once again momentarily at a loss for words. People really did suck. Including his parents. The mention of ID made him wonder for the first time where his was. The island was technically within American territory, but without his license, passport or credit cards, he was effectively imprisoned as much as Caden was.

"Let's try it this way," he continued because quizzing the slave was more comfortable than dwelling on his own situation. "What last name is on your birth certificate?"

"Beckett."

Now that he had the information, Tate realized it didn't get him anywhere. The questioning was really no more than a diversion, although if he was going to spend a lot of time with this guy, he wanted to know who he was living, and maybe fucking, with. "And how old are you?"

"Twenty."

Okay, age-compatible for the most part. At twenty-seven, Tate wasn't falling into the category of dirty old man if he used him for sex. And really, who was he kidding if he thought he wasn't going to. Not that he was obligated to use Caden in any sexual way. There was no one making him do so. He could simply relegate this slave to doing the icky stuff that Nurse Schmidt would absolutely do for him and which he *absolutely* didn't want her doing for him. Of course, Caden tending to him wouldn't be that much better. The whole dependency on others was a master class in humiliation.

Still, the slave was here and he'd obviously signed up for this so... "What are you supposed to do for me?" It was a stupid question, yet he wanted to be sure of Caden's view on his reason for being with him.

Caden shrugged. "Anything you want me to."

Tate tested that assertion. He flipped the covers over to expose his half-hard cock. "If I tell you to come over here and suck my dick...?"

"I don't think that's a good idea."

Tate felt a moment of disappointment, which was crazy because he was really just taking his frustration out on this kid, picking on him given that there was no one else to use as a pin cushion for his emotions. "Didn't you sell yourself as a sex slave?"

Caden nodded. "Yes, I did, but..."

"And you're supposed to obey me, right?"

"Yes."

"So, why are you refusing?"

Caden shifted his feet again, put his hand on his hip, dropped it again. "I'm not. It's just, you're not really in any kind of shape for a blow job."

"Oh? Says you?" Tate palmed his shaft and gave it a tug to harden it more. It was difficult to do so with his non-dominant hand. "Looks to me like I'm up for it."

"Yeah, except that you keep grimacing as if you're in pain. And you're making these little grunts, like the kind people make when something hurts but they're trying not to scream."

Tate narrowed his gaze. "No, I'm not." *Yes, I am.* Once again, how humiliating. That was going to be the watch word of the day for the next month, apparently. "Yeah, I'm in pain, okay? A nice orgasm will help relax me."

Caden shrugged. "If you say so…Tate."

The slave returned to the side of the bed, his nice tight package leading the way. Not that the kid was aroused or anything. It still looked as if a decent handful was being tightly constrained by the wisp of cotton he wore. Tate forced his gaze upward to the boy's face where there were other compelling things to focus on. Caden's lips were a blushing shade of pink, full and plump. They'd look lovely wrapped around Tate's cock. And just like that, a sufficient amount of blood rushed to his cock to make him achingly hard. His demand had turned into a real desire awfully quickly. He should feel guilty, maybe. Ashamed? Sure, except his anger overrode every other emotion. If this was what his parents thought would keep him pacified, he'd show them differently.

Caden stopped an inch from the edge of the bed. "How about a hand job?"

Tate glared at the boy. "How about you do what you're fucking told."

"Yes…Tate." The way Caden said his name as an honorific sounded ridiculous in the context, but there was no going back on that order now.

The slave put one knee on the bed in order to reach Tate with his mouth. Pain centers lit up all over Tate's body. He couldn't bite back the "Ow!"

Caden pushed off the bed again, not quite hiding a smirk.

When Tate thought he could speak coherently, he bit out, "Fine. I'll take the hand job. Good luck not touching the mattress." The smart-aleck remark was particularly idiotic given how he was the one who was going to regret the adverse effect.

The slave turned out to be both intelligent and flexible. He pumped some lotion from the bottle on the nightstand into his palm. Then, bracing his other arm against the metal headboard of Tate's hospital bed, he leaned over and took hold of Tate's dick. His touch was warm, his skin soft, and his grip firm enough to be arousing without being painful. Tate inhaled sharply, not from pain, this time, but from the spark of pleasure that shot into his balls. He caught Caden's scent, some kind of body spray, maybe. It smelled nice and displaced the antiseptic odor that had permeated his room even though he was no longer in the hospital.

It didn't take long or much effort to cause the climax to rip out of him. For a blessed moment, Tate knew only pleasure and joy as natural dopamine overrode all the physical and mental pain that were his constant companions these days. With a grunt and a sigh, Tate sank into his bed with his eyes closed.

He was aware that Caden moved away, heard water running, and didn't have the energy to so much as jump when a warm cloth was swiped over his dick.

Tired and satiated, Tate didn't fight the sleepiness that stole over him.

He snuggled into his pillows. "You're hired."

* * * *

When Tate next opened his eyes, the sun was setting, a fiery ball sinking beneath the waves. It really was a beautiful view. Calming. The second thing he saw was Caden sitting on a chair by the windows. He was reading a book with his head bent to give Tate a view of the top of his blond head. The guy still only wore his thong, probably because Tate hadn't given him leave to dress again. The realization that he now literally controlled another human being was both frightening and arousing. He'd always been a total top and loved his sex partners to be submissive in a non-BDSM sort of way. No real surprise there. Being a Graham gave him a natural desire to be in command. That usually meant making the first move on someone and picking up the tab. In bed, he liked to physically control his lovers, too, and be a little rough with them if they wanted him to be. Now, his situation with Caden literally meant issuing orders and getting his way in everything without any concern for what the other person might desire.

Wow, I could be a real monster—a real Graham—*if I don't rein myself in.*

"Hey." He'd meant it to be a casual call out. His tone was sharper than he'd intended, however.

Caden jerked and looked up before springing to his feet. He set his book down on the chair and came toward the bed with a weary and wary expression. "Yes, Tate?" On the surface, the slave's tone was neutral, but there was a detectable undercurrent of resentment.

Great. Well that fit perfectly with Tate's own mood because he needed to pee and he was never going to get used to doing that simple chore with the help of someone else. Which was nothing compared to having to take a shit. Thank God, people forgot what it was like to be a toddler, because having one's ass wiped by another made him want to fall into the blessed oblivion of unconsciousness. But there would be time to obsess over that mortification later. First things first.

Tate glared at his slave. "I need to take a leak."

Caden's eyes widened briefly as he looked around. "Umm, how do we do that?"

Tate didn't hide his exasperation. "Didn't they teach you anything?"

"No, actually. Nothing at all."

That answer took the wind of out Tate's resentment sails. Not that he'd given this whole debt slave issue more than a passing *Jesus, people suck* thought, he would have expected for there to be some kind of training. Although, really what would that have involved for sex slaves — the proper technique for oral sex, or the best way to hide the fact that you loathe what your owner is doing?

Tate jerked his chin in the direction of the bathroom. "There's a plastic urinal in there." He dropped his head onto the pillow with a huff, telling himself that peeing in front of the guy who'd jerked an orgasm out of his dick was no big deal. He'd done it plenty of times with stay-over lovers. Somehow this situation was different. Needing this kind of help with someone he'd been intimate with emphasized how much his life was no longer under his control. *It's not going to be forever.* He had to focus on that fact or he'd end up screaming into his pillow.

Caden didn't hesitate to comply with this latest demand. Acting as Tate's nurse was more dignified than being his whore. The man needed help in his recovery and there was nothing degrading in helping in this way. He strode into the land of marble and gleaming silver fixtures, only momentarily distracted by its oversized opulence as he had been during his earlier foray into the bathroom. He made a beeline to the plastic container sitting on the counter. Picking it up, he understood how it functioned immediately and applauded the improved engineering of the traditional bed pan. All he'd have to do was stick Tate's cock into the opening, then empty it after the deed was done. Simple.

And it would be nothing like the hand job he'd given the guy earlier. He wouldn't have to grip the hard heat of the shaft, feeling it pulsing in his palm, straining for release, warm cum splashing over his fingers...fighting the disturbing urge to lick it off. Asshole Tate might be, it was still hot to jerk a man into an orgasm. Caden shook his head to get a grip on himself as he returned to the bedroom. He was not going to think in terms of pleasure because there was none to be had. This wasn't a relationship, or even a brief fling. Everything he was doing was a job, a chore, born from desperation. The last thing he needed was to appreciate the intimate tasks he was going to be forced into performing, especially when those thoughts were starting to have the usual effect on his anatomy. Dressed as he was in only a thong, his interest in his master would be obvious, and that would be the most degrading thing of all.

Caden walked over the other side of the bed, where Tate's good arm was, to gain access to his dick. The guy stared straight ahead, his expression telegraphing how much he hated what was about to happen. Oddly, the fact that the man wasn't gleeful about forcing Caden to touch his body in this clinical way made it easier on Caden. It was a reminder that neither of them had asked for this clusterfuck of a relationship. If he thought about it, it was the parents who were the real assholes, entirely to blame for everything. And…he'd have to be careful to hide his feelings about that when he was called to do the first of his daily check-ins with the Grahams. Caden flipped the sheet off Tate's lap and reached for the limp dick lying there.

Tate slapped his hand away. "I'll do that part. You just hold the bottle in place."

Caden was oddly disappointed that he wasn't going to be able to touch his master, but also relieved because he wasn't into water sports. He kept his gaze on the last of the beautiful sunset visible through the wall of windows as Tate stuck himself into the container and… Nothing. For long, long seconds, nothing happened. Other than the two of them breathing in and out and the faint sound of the ocean waves crashing, the room was silent. Caden did his best to be invisible and to show no signs of impatience. Even though men grew accustomed to using urinals right next to other guys, this was totally different. Far more intimate, and not in the playful way that could happen after sex, with jockeying for a spot in front of the toilet. He couldn't help feeling sorry for Tate. And for himself. His life as a slave wasn't going to change no matter how much empathy he felt for this injured man.

Just as he was thinking about how he might prop up the container so that he could leave and give Tate the privacy he obviously needed, the sound of liquid hitting the plastic confirmed he wouldn't have to do that. Once he got started, Tate made short work of peeing. It was over in seconds and as soon as the man pulled his dick free, Caden marched his not-so-fragrant burden into the bathroom. Emptying it into the toilet and washing it out was easy enough. Really, if he thought about it, this was a piece of cake compared to what was surely coming later in the day, or the following morning at the latest. Use of the bed pan would come next. Nature in all its messiness wouldn't be denied. There was no point in dwelling on that, however, so he returned to the bedroom to await further orders.

God, this sucked on so many levels. He really should at least try to think of this as helping out a friend who'd been in a terrible accident and needed care. Instead of the fact that he was nothing more than a living piece of furniture for a spoiled brat, and a spy to boot. He really had no idea what he was supposed to tell the Grahams about their son. Were they interested in his recovery progress? That information surely came from the nurse. Did they expect him to tattle on everything Tate said about them? He wasn't going to do that. Although he was a slave now, he had some standards. He'd simply lie about that if they asked. Maybe they wanted the salacious details of how Tate used his body. That might be fun, actually, seeing how uncomfortable he could make them with a blow-by-blow description, sort to speak.

If he thought about it too much, he really resented being put in the position of a spy more than being a sex toy Hand jobs and blow jobs were already something he did voluntarily and enjoyed. There was little point in being upset about having to do it as a job. And as

Tate got better, Caden would turn into a blow-up doll so that his master didn't grow bored during the final stage of his recuperation. That latter bit might not be so bad. He did like it when a man took control and fucked him hard. Tate was appealing, too, when he wasn't being such an asshole. If he stopped taking out his resentments on Caden, they might have fun together. He put aside all his concerns as soon as he saw Tate, covered once more, but also pale and obviously in pain.

Caden approached the bed with a frown. "Is it time for your pain meds?"

Tate grimaced. "Probably. I'm not taking them, though."

"Why not?" The question popped out of Caden's mouth before he could think better of it. The man had not appreciated being challenged before.

Tate shot him an angry look. "Not that it's any of your business, but I don't like how they make me feel. My head gets fuzzy and I can't think straight. I get sleepy and crash like a two year old who's had too much sugar."

The vulnerability of the statement caught Caden by surprise. "So? What's the problem with that? It's not like you have to stay alert. I mean, you're safe here."

"Am I?" Tate's face was screwed up with anger, which seemed to be his default emotion.

Caden shrugged, trying to be casual in the face of such fury and…fear, almost. "Of course you are. I'm no threat, and neither is the nurse or Miss Ophelia, I'm assuming. I can check under the bed and behind the curtains for assassins if it will make you feel better." Even as he was throwing that bit of snark, he couldn't help wondering if there really was a danger to Tate on this island that he didn't know about.

Tate's eyes popped with an implied "you didn't just dare to mock me, did you?" when there was a sharp rap on the door that cut off any further response.

It opened to Miss Ophelia and another woman rolling a cart with two domed plates and the obvious accoutrements of dinner. Seeing and smelling it all made Caden realize long it had been since he'd last eaten.

"Good evening, Mr. Tate. Caden."

Caden instinctively hurried to stand behind the back of the chair he'd been curled up in only a short while ago, embarrassed to be so scantily dressed in front of the two women. He supposed he should be grateful not to be entirely naked. And, he realized with a sudden drop in his stomach, that he no longer had the luxury of privacy. If Tate ordered him to prance around the place with his body on full display, he had no choice but to obey, his own feelings be damned.

The housekeeper gave them both a wide smile and stood aside so that the other woman could settle the trolley next to the head of the bed, close enough for Tate to reach it with his good hand if he wanted.

Not that he had to. Miss Ophelia stepped over and dismissed the servant with a wave. She then pulled a folded bed tray out from under the cart and settled it over Tate's lap. She helped him sit up a little straighter before she placed a plate of white fish, jasmine rice and grilled vegetables on the tray. Everything had been cut into bite-sized pieces.

The woman stood back. "There are you. The Mahi Mahi was caught fresh today. The rice has saffron in it, and Cook used some jerk seasoning on the squash. There's mango bread pudding if you're interested in dessert." The woman glanced at Caden. "There's a portion for you too, naturally." She lifted the remaining dome to expose a plate identical to Tate's.

"Thank you."

Caden was genuinely grateful. He hadn't known what he was going to be given to eat but he hadn't expected to be fed the same thing as his master. As he approached the cart, he saw that his food was also cut up. Well, that was convenient, he supposed, and might make Tate feel a little less like a child about his meal preparation. The alternative was that they didn't trust Caden with a knife, and given Tate's provocatively foul mood, that was perhaps not an unfounded concern.

"Later this evening, Caden, I'll come to take you to my quarters. Mr. Graham wants a video conference daily and you can use my tablet for it."

"Mata Hari," Tate muttered.

Caden ignored the dig if only because it was true. "Thank you, ma'am."

He waited for Miss Ophelia to leave before picking up his plate and fork and digging in. He paused with the food halfway to his mouth, realizing that maybe he needed permission... Christ, this whole debt slave thing was confusing. The agent had told him that his owner would set the ground rules, but so far, other than forcing him to disrobe, Tate had done nothing of the kind.

Caden stayed in that ridiculous position for a few seconds before Tate noticed.

Chewing his mouthful, the guy rolled his eyes. "What, are you waiting for permission to eat or something?"

Caden nodded, once again embarrassed and resentful and feeling even more overwhelmed with his new status than he had when he'd first walked into the Grahams' home.

"Eat. Now and whenever you want. I don't want to have to look after you like you're a baby or something."

Caden shoved the food into his mouth before he could say something really stupid, like *I'm not the baby in this room.*

They ate in silence for a minute or two. Dinner really was delicious, and the staff had probably just assumed he got the same food as this master, so he didn't have to worry about eating dog food for the next ten years. Or, at least while he was on the island. He had no idea what his fate would be once Tate had fully recovered. As there was nothing he could do about it, he forced the worry from his mind.

Tate made an exasperated sounding noise. "Don't just stand there. Go get that chair you were hiding behind or something. *God.*" Once again, this man acted as if it were Caden's idea that he be there, as if he had imposed himself upon Tate.

Talking back, defending himself from the unwarranted anger, wasn't going to help anything. So he wordlessly put his plate back on the trolley and went to lug a chair seated at a small desk that seemed far lighter than the massive one that had hidden his lower half. He sat down and primly went back to eating, not bothering to look at Tate. The guy seemed fine feeding himself, except—crap—there was a glass of iced tea on the trolley with a straw sticking out of it, which technically was within Tate's reach but probably would spill if he tried to pick it up, given how the tray had him hemmed in.

Suppressing a sigh, Caden put his plate down again and picked up the glass. "Would you like some?"

Tate hesitated, clearly wanting to refuse, but he nodded once instead. Caden pushed the trolley out of his way before leaning over to press the straw against

Tate's lips. He had to stare at the man's face in order not to botch the job and there was no denying that Tate was a stone cold eleven on the sexy man scale. There were lots of angular shapes and a strong, straight nose. There was also a few days' worth of scruff, which only served to make him the perfect picture of some kind of action movie hero. Days of being in bed made his short, dark hair stand up in crazy patterns, but that only added to the fuckability of the man. If Tate were about a decade older, he would have been Caden's go-to wet dream. Then again, look where that daddy fetish had landed him.

Here. In debt up to his eyeballs, while also penniless and friendless because Andrew had succeeded in isolating him as part of his controlling behavior. Dumb kid that Caden had been, he'd thought it was merely the older, sophisticated man helping him jettison his immature posse. He hadn't realized the true effect until he'd tried reaching out to people he'd used to know when his world had come crashing down. It turned out that he'd also picked lousy friends to begin with, and ghosting someone didn't lead to easy forgiveness. He'd been an idiot in so many ways, and now he was reaping the punishment of it.

I'm getting just what I deserve.

Tate had to jerk away when he was finished drinking because Caden had been too lost in his thoughts to pay attention. He shot a glare at Caden before returning to his plate of food.

"Sorry." Caden took his seat and picked up his glass of iced tea, the one that didn't have a straw because he wasn't the one with a broken collarbone and busted leg and…whatever else had broken when Tate had…what had Harding said about it on the plane? Oh yeah, something about slamming face first into a tree.

They finished the meal in silence. Tate refused the dessert, which was a shame because mango bread pudding sounded delicious. If the master wasn't eating, Caden figured he shouldn't, either, regardless of what Tate had said about suiting himself eating-wise. He piled the dirty remnants of the meal onto the cart and wheeled it into the sitting room. Someone would come for it eventually, and as he wasn't sure where or how the intercom system worked, he simply returned to the bedroom, shutting himself in with his master.

Tate said nothing. He merely lay there, staring at the ceiling. Tightness around his mouth exposed the pain he had to be in. Stubborn as his master was, Caden decided to take charge of the issue. The medication chart was hanging on the wall above the nightstand. A quick scan confirmed that Tate was way overdue on his pain pills. Caden quickly located the bottle he needed among the many that were there, all lined up like soldiers ready for duty. And man, there were a lot of them. Caden didn't even recognize many of the names, but he'd have to learn what each one did and follow the chart because God knew, Tate didn't seem inclined to educate him. Calling the nurse in was a distinct possibility, but he figured her intrusion would simply agitate the patient and that wasn't going to be helpful for any of them.

Caden shook out a pill and filled the adult version of a sippy cup with fresh water. He held both out to Tate. "Here."

Tate gave him the side-eye. "I've already told you how I feel about taking that shit."

"Yes, Tate, you did. And I reassured you that you're not in Dr. Evil's lair, so you don't need to worry about staying alert." He pushed the pill against the man's lips. "Seriously, who's this stubborn refusal helping?"

A half-second later, Tate opened his mouth, took the pill and swallowed down some water when Caden pressed the straw into him. "I hate this," he said once he was done.

"I'm sure you do. Anyone would." Caden put the cup down and scanned the chart of see what needed to be given and when for the rest of the evening. "What do you want to do, watch some TV?"

Tate sighed, but the lines of pain were already smoothing out. "I guess. Put on ESPN."

Oh goody, sports. Caden's not so favorite thing to watch. This wasn't a democracy, however, so he hunted out the remote and turned on the million-inch TV bolted to the wall opposite the bed. The island had satellite, so there were endless channels to pick from. But his master wanted to watch men chase a ball or something around somewhere. Sitting back into his chair, Caden gave him exactly what he wanted.

Chapter Three

Tate burst out of his nightmare with a gasp and tried to bolt upright before flares of pain throughout his body reminded him that he couldn't do that at the moment. He lay back against the pillows of his hospital bed in the gloom of his bedroom. A bit of light was seeping past the edges of the curtain so he could tell it was dawn. He swallowed hard to push down the horrible memories that had made him wake in a cold sweat. This wasn't anything new, and it had nothing to do with his skiing accident. No, this kind of nightmare dated to the other time he'd landed in the hospital.

He blinked hard to steady himself and come fully awake. God, he needed to pee and didn't even remember falling asleep. *Fucking pain pills.* And that reminded him of who had been the one to push the damn things on him. Where the hell was his slave? Probably bedding down on the couch in the sitting room because no one, including himself, had considered where the boy would sleep. Or maybe the servants thought Caden would share his bed, which was stupid, because it was only designed for one person. And not to mention how he alone caused himself a lot of pain just by moving a few inches here or there. *God.* He'd have to tell Miss Ophelia to have a cot brought in. There was no point in having a slave if he wasn't going to be conveniently nearby.

Tate took a deep breath to be heard through the door. "Caden!"

"What?" A head popped up in Tate's peripheral vision. The slave was sleeping on the floor, apparently.

Tate strained to get a better look and yup, there was a blanket and a pillow and a pretty boy with not-quite-a-bed head. And when Caden stood, there was his other head, sticking out of his thong from morning wood because of course, Tate hadn't given him permission to get dressed again. And whose fault was that? Tate had told Caden that the pain meds made him loopy.

Caden blinked at him. "What do you need...Tate?"

Tate forced himself to stare into the kid's eyes. "Urinal. Now." That was as much as he could get out with his mind still picturing Caden's erection.

His slave hurried to the bathroom, flashing Tate with his naked butt. God, thongs were sexy. Rudi Gernreich should have received the Presidential Medal of Freedom for his innovation, even if it had been designed with women in mind. At least, that's what he assumed the man let people think. But surely old Rudi had to have pictured someone like Caden sporting the sexy look, as well. That slender piece of fabric riding between Caden's ass cheeks was like a beacon. *Follow me. With your dick.* By the time the slave had returned, Tate was embarrassingly hard and no longer simply because of a full bladder.

Peeing with an erection was tricky under the best of circumstances. Having to stick it into a plastic hole was comical in its level of difficulty. Tate tried his best to make short work of it, keeping his gaze on his efforts and not on how his slave was reacting to the struggle. There was a brief snort that turned into a cough when Tate flashed his eyes in Caden's direction. The kid was staring off at some unseen spot on the other side of the room with an expression that didn't quite hide his mirth. As he finally got his cock into the urinal, Tate allowed himself the right to stare at his new acquisition. Caden was beautiful. There was no denying that. There couldn't be too many people who would be able to avoid looking a little longer than necessary at that heart-shaped face with high cheekbones, long thick lashes and plumped bow lips. His pale skin was smooth and his muscles toned. Tate could imagine spending hours running his fingers over that flesh.

And those thoughts were not helping with his current situation.

Closing his eyes, Tate relaxed against his pillow and finally — finally — his bladder released itself. It was embarrassing, which was odd. Tate hadn't felt quite as much so when Nurse Ratched had been helping him. There was something about being helpless with such a simple bodily function in front of somebody he was hot for that caused his cheeks to heat. That never happened to him. Not since adulthood, anyway. When he was done, he kept his eyes closed and let Caden take care of the disembarking by removing the urinal.

Noises emanating from the bathroom for long minutes told him that Caden had cleaned up and probably relieved himself. He couldn't help picturing the boy taking his own dick in his hand, pulling the thong back into place, washing his hands and maybe his face. Those thoughts led to ones involving the slave showering, soap suds flowing down his silky, pale skin. Did Caden jerk off in the shower? Most guys did. And what would that look like? The boy's lovely face screwed up with the effort to wring an orgasm out of his balls. And these images were not helping him relax. He needed to cut this shit out — now — for the sake of his sanity.

Tate opened his eyes at the sound of the slave returning to the bedroom. Damn, but the boy's dick was safely tucked into the thong. Had the guy jerked off while out of sight even without taking a shower, or was it merely the effect of peeing? Tate frowned when he realized he wasn't sure how long Caden had been out of sight. *Damn pain pills*. There were probably at fault for his daydreaming about his slave's enticing body, too. They were still messing with his head. He was so done taking them, no matter how insistent Caden became.

Tate opened his mouth to say…something. The door opened abruptly, cutting off any effort to do so. The nurse strode in with her usual brisk efficiency and lack of knocking. She acted like he was a coma patient in a hospital, entitled to no privacy. Miss Ophelia and one of the other servants entered in her wake with a breakfast trolley. Thank God he was done with the urinal already. A sudden audience to his efforts would have caused the pee to back up into his body with humiliation. The timing of their arrival was nearly perfect. Too much so? He glanced around the room, not for the first time wondering if there was surveillance on him because yes, his parents were that much of controlling psychopaths.

He forced himself to stop thinking about how trapped he was and focused on Nurse Schmidt instead.

"You're still here?" It was a dumb question. He was still an *invalid* and needed medical oversight.

The woman barely spared him a glance as she rolled over to the side of his bed her instruments of torture. Well, that was ridiculous hyperbole. Having temperature, blood oxygen levels and blood pressure taken was a quick, painless affair. His vital signs were perfect, which came as no surprise to him. But Schmidt duly noted the numbers in her tablet, as if the information were of critical importance. Then she started in on the tougher stuff, checking the status of his leg and collarbone, poking and prodding to confirm nothing had necrotized before cleaning and rebandaging. If his injuries had stayed inside his body instead of bursting through his skin, his aftercare would have been easier. Sadly, in addition to being in traction and a shoulder sling, he had a few dozen stitches that had to be dealt with. He always forced himself to watch everything in order to be sure to remember what not to do once he was free. He'd come to accept that he had to dial back on his risk-taking. Death didn't worry him, but this? He hated the dependency on others and if he weren't more careful, he could end up permanently in this condition—confined to his bed and with his body no longer under his control.

Everything the nurse did hurt like a bitch. With gritted teeth, he uttered no sound to confirm that to anyone. He was probably fooling no one. Still, he had to try. As soon as the nurse finished by adjusting the methods of his confinement to make sure they were in place properly, he let out a long, slow breath. He dared to look at Caden, who stood away from the bed, and saw something like sympathy in the boy's eyes. Tate hated that expression and emotion being directed at him.

"What are you looking at?" He spit out the question with a harshness that he instantly regretted.

It had the desired effect, however. Caden lowered his gaze. "Nothing." Without saying more, the boy picked up the pillow and blanket he'd used on the floor and quickly returned them to the closet.

Tate couldn't help following the slave's movements. There was a grace and dignity to the boy. It indicated that Caden had been born into security with a high degree of self-worth that came from not having to scratch and scramble to survive. Thinking that, he wondered once more how Caden had ended up as a debt slave. And of course, the physical attraction remained. Not even the spike in pain from the nurse's efforts stopped him from wanting the boy. He used his free hand to squash his burgeoning erection. If the nurse noticed the change in his physical condition, she was wise enough to say nothing. With her usual stern demeanor, she forced his daily non-narcotic medication on him. He swallowed them without hesitation or complaint. The sooner they finished, the sooner the women would leave.

"Everything is healing well. I'll be back before dinner." Schimdt's crisp words were followed by her departure.

Then it was Miss Ophelia's turn. She gestured for the trolley to be brought closer to the bed and served him his breakfast herself, as she'd habitually done. From his childhood, the woman had always acted more like a nanny than a house manager whenever he'd been on the island. He felt close to her, which was why it stung all the more that she was helping his parents keep him prisoner.

"Yogurt, fruit and granola," she said as she mixed the ingredients into a bowl. "And Cook made croissants this morning."

Tate's attention was half on the food in front of him and half on Caden maneuvering his chair next to the trolley. Once again, he noticed that for a slave, Caden had a lot of...poise, he supposed was the right description. Not that he thought people in his position should be cowering or anything. He just figured that it would be humbling to be owned, even for a limited time, by someone else. When he looked into Caden's eyes, however, he saw mostly resentment. And who could blame the kid? Tate himself was plenty resentful of how his life had turned out and he was still a free man. Sort of.

Before Caden could sit his bare ass on the chair, Tate felt a spurt of shame over forcing the guy to parade around others almost nude. He hadn't missed how the kid had hidden behind a chair the previous night when the women had entered. Nor was he unaware of the fact that Caden hadn't even tried this morning, trapped as he was caring for Tate.

"Put your pants back on." Once again, he hadn't meant to be so sharp, as if he were mad at the boy. Well, he *was* mad, but no more than he was at everyone else. Even so...

Caden actually jumped before complying. He slowly went to fetch his jeans and as he shoved first one leg, then the other into them, he eyed Tate with unconcealed resentment. "Shall I put my T-shirt on too...*Tate*?"

Yeah, Caden was really calling him out in a passive-aggressive way about how Tate wanted to pretend he wasn't a slave-owner while also ordering him around...exactly as if he owned him.

Picking up his spoon, Tate said, "No." Because apparently he was an asshole. He wanted something pretty and distracting to gaze at and Caden's naked and hairless chest with pert nipples fit the bill. Tate shoveled some yogurt into his mouth and crunched his way through the pieces of granola as he continued to stare at the boy.

Miss Ophelia sighed quietly and shook her head at him. Then she smiled at Caden. "There's enough of the healthy stuff for you too, but you'll find some French toast under the domed plate. A boy your age needs a hearty breakfast."

Tate swallowed hard. "Hey, I'm not much older. Where's my French toast?"

Miss Ophelia gave him the evil eye. "Your treat is the croissants. Get out of this bed and start moving around, then we can up your calorie count."

"What are you, my trainer?" Tate allowed his bitterness to come through.

"No. I'm your keeper. Neither of us is happy about it, but that's how it is. Now behave yourself."

Tate was momentarily stunned by those honest words.

"You know," Caden said as he sat. "The more compliant you are with the medical restrictions, the faster you'll regain your freedom." He lifted the dome of his plate to reveal a delicious meal that included bacon along with the French toast.

Tate glared at him as he scooped up more yogurt. "Your opinion was not requested." He felt like an ass the moment the words came out of his mouth. There was no taking them back, however, so he shut himself up with food.

* * * *

"Hey, come here."

Caden looked up from his book at the sound of his master's voice. No matter what Tate wanted to be called, he was his owner. God, the guy ran hot and cold, demanding and mean at times and almost kind in others. If Caden weren't careful, he'd get complacent around this man and then when the not-nice version of Tate leaped out, it would be harder to take. This was the perfect reminder to be vigilant. After a silent breakfast in which Tate's foul mood had been palpable, they'd spent the rest of the morning in relative companionship, watching more sports. Boring. But also doing a crossword puzzle, which had been kind of fun. Tate Graham was a smart guy, getting the clues right so quickly that there wasn't much of a challenge doing even the ones marked as hard. He'd seemed happier and relaxed during that time, then had turned back into an ogre when Miss Ophelia had brought him papers to review. Business shit, was what Tate had called them, before ordering Caden to throw them in the trash without even having looked at them.

Lunch had come soon after. No simple sandwiches in the Graham household. Grilled salmon with a soy-sauce-based glaze, honeyed carrots and fluffy whipped potatoes had comprised the meal. Plus, macadamia and white chocolate chip cookies had been provided and because Tate had eaten one, so had Caden. They had still been a bit warm, the benefit of being rich enough to have a private chef even in a vacation home. With rich food like this, he wondered whether he could use the gym that had to be in the house, or swim in the pool he'd spied when he'd arrived.

Once the meal was done, the inaugural and totally awkward bedpan event had finally happened. And as icky as that had been, he couldn't help noticing and admiring this master's physique. The man had *muscles*. You could bounce a quarter off that ass and send it into orbit. Because Caden's lovers—a pretty paltry three—had been older men, he'd never really appreciated the benefit of young, fit bodies. The sight of Tate's caused him to flash hot and that reaction was both disorientating and encouraging. He'd assumed he would hate servicing the guy, but now he had hope that it might have some elements of enjoyment.

Putting aside his book, Caden rose to comply with Tate's order. As he approached the bed, he kept his gaze on his master's face and tried not to think about what he'd seen when the nurse had done her duty. Because yikes. As hot as Tate was, he also looked like Frankenstein's monster's gorgeous younger brother. He'd assumed that it was just broken bones that he was recovering from, but the stitches he'd glimpsed were gruesome evidence that Tate's accident had been a fucking awful one. No surprise that even without taking his pain meds, the guy slept a lot. It was fine by Caden, of course. It gave him time to himself and with the view of the ocean and lots of good books to choose from, he was almost on vacation.

Almost.

There was a look in Tate's eyes, a hungry one. And when Caden reached the side of the bed, his master flicked off the covers to reveal that he'd woken aroused and needy.

"Take care of this."

Caden stared at the man's leaking cock. It was big, long and thick, with a vein bulging out from one side in testament to how rock hard the dick was. Big balls hugged tightly to his body and there was a tiny pearl of cum shining along the slit of his cockhead. Caden mentally licked his lips. He really did love giving head, and even choking himself on a big cock. Too bad Tate was really not in a condition for a blow job. They were both going to have to be satisfied with a repeat of the day before.

He pumped some of the nearby lotion into his palm to ease the way. It was awkward, but he got as close to the bed as he could without jostling it and reached out to clasp the shaft insistently waving to be touched. Tate's gaze skittered away and he closed his eyes as he settled back against his pillows. Caden had to brace himself by grabbing the metal headboard as he wrapped the fingers of his other hand around Tate's dick. The skin felt as taut as it looked and was warm to the point of being hot. Or maybe that was his imagination. Maybe it was he who was hot, sweat popping out all over him while he worked Tate's hard-on with a finesse that he knew he'd successfully cultivated over the last few years. The irony of his life was that despite resenting his predicament as a sex slave, Caden *liked* to be of service to his lovers. He craved catering to another man's needs. It made him feel wanted and, in a pathetic way that was simply a mirage, loved.

A psychologist would have a field day rummaging around in his brain. Dead mother he never knew, distant father who shuttled him between boarding school and sleepaway camp in order to not deal with him. Yeah, he'd been a Holdover kid for sure, and still felt sorry for himself because of it. He had daddy issues in a major way. There was no point in denying that truth to himself. And he'd found what he'd believed to be the perfect man to love him in a way he'd never been before. Too bad for him, Andrew had turned out to be way worse than Caden's father. At least the old man had left Caden with a small fortune instead of directing it to his younger wife. Andrew had done the opposite, leaving him right here, giving a spoiled guy a hand job.

It took very little effort or skill to get Tate off. Caden had barely managed a few strokes before the guy erupted with his head thrown back and his body going rigid. Caden was careful to follow through, stroking the twitching cock until the last spurt of cum dribbled down over his fingers. With a shudder and a groan, Tate went slack. It was impossible to tell if he'd fallen asleep or was just avoiding interaction with Caden anymore. It was possible that Tate was embarrassed about using Caden so crassly. He snorted to himself. *Yeah, right.* Guys like Tate didn't worry about how others felt. Caden had known lots of boys like him at school. They were selfish pricks and he'd do well to remember that he wasn't a friend or a guest. He was a slave.

He released the cock and hurried to the bathroom to wash up. There was a surprising ache in his balls and tingling in his own dick over the experience. He looked at himself in the mirror over the sink as he turned on the water. His cheeks were flushed and his pupils blown, which was crazy. This hadn't been sex. This had been a job. Still, he couldn't resist again his impulse to taste, licking a small amount of cum off a finger before he plunged his hands down to wash. The flavor of Tate bursting across his tongue was an unsurprising salty and bitter one. He shouldn't have liked it, but he'd always enjoyed dining on cum, savoring and swallowing what he'd sucked out of a man.

This was different, though. *Right?* It was like enjoying chocolates on a job where you had to wrap them up for endless hours on an assembly line. One should grow sick of it just because it had become boring duty. And yet, as he wet a cloth, there was no denying that he was completely aroused. Good thing Tate had allowed him to put on his jeans. It wouldn't do for his non-master "*call me Tate*" to know that Caden was attracted to him. That would probably give the fucker too much satisfaction, and feed an ego that needed no encouragement.

When he returned to the bedroom, Tate's eyes were open. He watched Caden as he came over and gently wiped the guy's dick. Caden could feel Tate's gaze on him, and when he straightened, he saw that Tate was staring at Caden's crotch. Or rather, the way his hard dick was pressing against the worn material of his jeans.

"Take off your pants." The command was delivered in a casual, almost teasing way.

Caden couldn't help shaking his head and backing away.

"Do it!" The harsh tone of the order burned away the friendlier version.

Caden narrowed his gaze and didn't try to hide his anger over the order. "Yes. *Master*." The fucker wasn't going to get away with treating him like a slave while pretending that he didn't own him.

Tate didn't bother to correct him. It was possible he wasn't even listening to anything at all. The intensity of his gaze as he watched Caden strip off his pants was surely stealing from his other senses. The guy's breathing became harsh, his chest rising and falling more quickly. His nostrils flared and he even gnawed at his lower lip.

Okay, so Tate Graham wanted him. What a surprise? That had been the idea all along. His parents' scheme depended on Caden to make their son happy and complacent, to somehow forget that he was trapped by them. This was a good thing, because he didn't want those people to be mad at *him* and sell him on to God knew who. At least being with Tate was an easy gig.

Tate shook his head once when Caden stopped with his underwear on. "All of it."

Hooking his thumb on the waistband, Caden shoved his thong down and stepped out of it. His cock burst out at full arousal. He knew what Tate saw — a slender and pretty dick, not huge but a good mouthful. Or so Andrew had always said. He wasn't going to think of that asshole, though. Nothing would kill his erection faster. Although, maybe that would be a good thing…?

"Getting me off did that to you, huh?"

Caden was surprised by that statement. "Well, sure. I mean I *am* gay, so like other guys' dicks and giving hand jobs even when I don't have a choice." He shrugged as if defining his sexual orientation to another man whom he knew to be gay, too, wasn't weird.

Tate continued to stare at his cock. "I wasn't sure if you were. Someone in a financial bind like you are would probably agree to anything."

Financial bind? Sure, that was one way of putting it. Did someone like Tate even understand what it was like to not have money, to be in debt up to their eyeballs? Probably not. Caden hadn't given those unrich people around him much thought at all. It was only with his new-found *bind*, that he understood what the vast majority of people had to deal with moneywise.

"Jerk yourself off."

The order didn't really surprise Caden. It wasn't as if Tate was going to reciprocate with the hand job. Even if he wanted to, his injuries didn't permit too much movement.

Caden decided right then that he may as well do this right and get something out of it. Other than the requisite orgasm, that was. He put the cloth on the nightstand and grabbed hold of his dick with one hand while cupping his balls with his other. With his legs braced, he got to work, keeping his eyes on Tate. Not that it mattered where he looked, because the guy was staring at what was happening below the belt. He even turned a little to face Caden more squarely, undoubtedly ignoring the bit of pain that came from the movement.

Caden didn't bother with any lotion. He didn't need it, liking the harshness of jerking dry skin. Besides, it didn't take long before he started leaking pre-cum. It was a quirk of his physiology that he lubricated himself a lot prior to the finale, as if his balls were so overloaded with cum that they needed to release the pressure immediately. Soon, his shaft was slick enough to make the glide of his fingers up and down fast and easy. As he hit the top, he swiped his thumb through his slit. He wasn't a pain slut, not really, but he still liked a little bite to his sex to increase his pleasure. When he was going solo, he made liberal use of his fingernails on both his cock and his balls. He squeezed his hands and dug into the tender skin.

It didn't take long for the pressure to build to the point of eruption. He clamped down on the bottom of his shaft to hold the climax back. The edging was fun, but it was also amusing to see the look for frustration on Tate's face. *That's right, asshole. You're going to have to wait until I'm good and ready for you to get your eyeful.* Caden had no power in his new life as a slave. He knew and accepted it—mostly. This was one thing about himself that he could control. He brought himself close a few more times before finally letting go. With a long moan that he didn't try to hold back, Caden came with a blinding intensity. He'd intended to keep watching Tate but it proved to be impossible. His eyes slammed shut and he threw his head back. His knees nearly buckled. He only just managed to keep to his feet.

And when it was over, he stood panting, slowly coming back to himself and with his brain function returning, he realized he'd forgotten to use the washcloth to catch his cum. He lunged for it, and while he did contain a lot of his cum before it dribbled onto the carpet, some of it still dripped by his toes.

"Shit." Caden raced to the bathroom, cleaned himself up and returned with a refreshed cloth. He knelt down and started rubbing.

"That was totally hot."

Caden looked up in surprise. Tate's expression was smoldering. There were no other words to describe it. Caden paused in his cleaning efforts and sat back on his heels. He didn't know how to respond.

"You don't have to do that. The maid can clean it."

Caden grimaced. "As if I want some poor woman dealing with my cum. And I am a slave after all, so…"

Tate flicked his still exposed dick. "If I weren't a fucking invalid, this boy would be back in action and pounding into your ass." He grimaced and sighed while laying the sheet back over his lap. "I really hate this."

Caden had no trouble believing that. He returned to cleaning up his mess and wondered if the smell would linger. "Try a safer sport next time. Like pickleball."

Tate actually barked out a laugh at that. "Sure. Or sailing. How about that? Sailing around on a lake is pretty safe, right? Until it's not."

Caden stopped again. He had no idea why that observation had been laced with such bitterness. There was something he was missing, something he didn't know. The Graham family had always been on a whole other level of wealth from his own. He'd heard the name but didn't really know much about them. Except that he'd paid enough attention to the gossip sites to know that Tate was often mentioned in them, although usually in regard to sports, so nothing he was interested in reading about. It was on the tip of his tongue to ask what Tate had meant. Then he remembered that he was a slave and it was none of his business.

With a grunt, Tate closed his eyes. "Get dressed when you've finished there and open a window, for God's sake. I don't want Miss Ophelia to be offended."

Any more than she should be by the fact that I'm here as your slave? Of course, he said nothing of the kind out loud. He merely continued with his task, more relaxed than he should have been.

Chapter Four

Tate poked at his dinner. Pain took his appetite away but it was far better than the fogginess induced by the meds everyone kept trying to push on him. The good way to distract himself from it was to watch his slave chowing down with the gusto that only someone still holding onto a teenage metabolism could possess. Even this mundane task was enticing, with Caden's blond-haired head bowed down as he shoveled in his food. Not that the boy lacked table manners. He knew what fork to use because yes, Cook had decided that serving a formal multi-course meal was the best way to cheer up the patient. No bits or pieces fell to the floor or covered Caden's chin. The guy sat with his linen napkin draped over his thigh and used it now and then to dab at the corners of his pretty mouth. That was the best spot Tate had to look at, given that the boy had taken his order to cover up to the extent that he wore his shirt as well as his jeans. *Pity, that.* His naked torso would have been the ultimate distraction from everything that sucked in Tate's life at the moment.

Yes, Mumsy and Daddy, Mater and Pater, the twin servant imps of Satan, Mr. and Mrs. Clifford J. Graham III, also known as his psychopathically controlling parents knew him too well. They had purchased the perfect distraction for him to a degree that he had to acknowledge made him truly fucked. It was going to be impossible to hang onto his resentment about his predicament when he couldn't keep resisting the allure of Caden. The slave had him in a perpetual state of semi if not full arousal, which was a good sign if he thought about it. His body had to be on the mend if it could afford to have a major amount of its blood supply concentrated in his dick. And it had only been what, a day? *I am so screwed.*

He pushed at his tray like a petulant child. "I'm done. Take this away."

Putting both his fork and his napkin down, Caden jumped to his feet and hurried to comply. He stared at Tate's plate. "You didn't eat much."

"I'm not hungry. A problem you don't have, apparently. Feel free to eat my dinner. I'm sure all of this food is better than what you're used to." God, he was being so bitchy, but he couldn't help it. Caden was the only available target for his ire.

Caden actually scraped the remnants of Tate's meal onto his own plate before sitting again. "Well, the pork was a little overdone. Not that I'd ever complain or anything. The cook was probably having an off day." He flicked his gaze toward Tate. "We all have them."

Tate bunched the sheet up around his lap to hide how much more he'd become aroused. "Yup, we do. And you'd know that better than most, wouldn't you? I mean you must have had a shit ton of *bad days* to crash yourself in the land of the debt slaves. You really don't have a right to complain about anything at the moment."

Caden narrowed his gaze at Tate as he chewed and swallowed. "You're right. I totally fucked myself. Unlike you, who was kidnapped and thrown out of a helicopter against your will onto some kind of gazillianth black diamond run by unrepentant evil-doers. Oh wait, I forgot. You did that stupid thing all by yourself, and I bet you paid through the nose for the experience. It must have really sucked for you when you realized, just before slamming into a tree, that your life choices had been abysmal."

Tate knew he had no business being pissed. He still couldn't help sitting up and saying, "Shut. Up."

Caden tossed his fork and napkin onto the trolley. "Make. Me."

Tate actually sputtered for a few seconds, his mind scrambling to make sense of what his slave had just said to him. "I'm sorry. Do you not understand that I own you?"

Caden stood, eyes flashing, lips in a grim line, his slender chest heaving with each breath. "*You* don't own me. Your parents do, and I'm following their orders to the T."

Tate was once more stunned into silence for a few seconds. It wasn't what Caden had said—which was true. It was more that this adorable and sexy version of Caden was totally distracting. He wanted this guy so badly it overrode everything else his body was feeling. And understanding how enthralled he was becoming to this slave who was also a spy infuriated him.

"Put the trolley out in the sitting room, then take off all of your clothes. If this little rebellion of yours continues, I will complain to my parents and demand a replacement and how will that work out for you?"

He caught the flash of fear in Caden's eyes and immediately hated himself for issuing the threat. But it was working. Caden removed the remnants of the meal and returned in short order. With his gaze fixed on the carpet, he stripped down to his skin and stood waiting for Tate's next orders. The guy seemed to be trembling slightly, although whether it was because he was scared or furious, it was impossible to tell. Some of each, probably.

Tate was disgusted by himself, yet more than that, he craved this boy. He wanted to touch him all over, run his fingers along all that silky-looking skin. He beckoned with his free hand. "Come here," he added when he remembered that Caden wasn't looking at him.

Caden came over to the side of the bed, his expression shuttered.

"Closer."

"I don't want to bump the bed." The boy's tone was neutral, as if he were trying to stay above the tension between them.

"Let me worry about that."

Caden closed the gap between himself and the edge of the bed, managing to not quite touch it.

Tate reached a little farther than was comfortable but he ignored his body's protest to clasp the slave's hip. It was as he expected, smooth and warm. A shiver vibrated against his touch and a small puff of air passed Caden's lips. Encouraged that this attraction wasn't one-sided, Tate slid his fingers back to cup one firm butt cheek. He used the hold as leverage to tug the boy even closer. With a gasp, Caden shot out a hand to steady himself on the headboard. His other hand hovered over Tate's uninjured leg for a second before gravity forced him to lean on it so as not to sprawl across Tate's lap.

The contact jarred his body enough to make him grunt and for a few seconds, they both took in harsh breaths.

Caden grimaced. "You should let me stand back."

"No. We're both enjoying this too much."

He wasn't trying to bait the slave. The boy's hard cock bobbed over the tent his own erection was making under the sheet.

"It can't be good for you."

"On the contrary, it's the best medicine I can take right now. And if we're going to be stuck with each other, we may as well have some fun."

Tate slid his finger past the slave's crack to press against his hole. Now, the boy moaned and his grip on Tate's thigh tightened. He really should have pulled away enough to lotion up, but Tate couldn't quite control himself. Instead, he pushed past the puckered ring, which unfolded with little resistance, welcoming him inside the slave's snug channel. He pushed as far as his finger could go, happy to reach the ridged flesh he knew would literally push Caden's button.

"Oh fuck." The slave jerked his hips and clenched his hole.

Tate smiled as he stroked the prostate. "You like that, huh?"

"You know I do," Caden answered through gritted teeth. He stared down at him. "Keep that up and I'm going to come all over your sheets."

Tate stilled his finger. "We can't have that. Free my cock and jerk it with yours."

There was a flash of something like a smile in the slave's eyes before he lifted his hand to pull down the sheet. Tate's dick was there, waiting for him and eager to participate. Caden had to place his knee upon the bed in order to clasp both his cock and Tate's in one hand. He couldn't encircle them completely, of course, but his grip was enough to rub them together in a clumsy, yet wholly successful, manner.

The surprisingly intense pleasure from the contact overrode the pain spurred by the jostling. Tate threw caution to the wind and bucked his hips into Caden's hold in time to the thrusting he started with his finger. He forced his eyes to stay open so he could watch the slave's face as the orgasm quickly built then tore through the boy. His own rapidly followed, sending his eyelids crashing down and him flying on a cloud of pure bliss. For a few exquisite moments, he knew no pain, not physical or emotional. His life converged on this singular, joyful event, shared between him and this boy. Their forced circumstances didn't dampen the experience at all. Not even after he came back into himself.

His first instinct when he returned to reality and the pain that his exertion had caused was to be angry and lash out. He stopped himself because Caden's face was right there in front of him. Beautiful, with cheeks flushed from the shared pleasure, but also with a hint of sadness in the expression. Pushing aside his resentment over his own situation, he focused on that of the slave's. Taking his feelings out on the boy was not only unfair, it didn't help either of them. To a large degree, they were in this together. Better to cultivate at least a détente and maybe they could both emerge from this entrapment unscathed. Tate gently removed his finger, grinning when Caden's hole squeezed to keep it inside.

"We both could use some cleaning up in case someone comes in. The nurse is unpredictable sometimes, and a real dragon."

Caden let go of their dicks, his fingers coated in cum, and stood back from the bed. There was something utterly hot about how their fluids mingled. Tate wanted to demand a taste. But no, that seemed like too much at the moment. Being kinder to the slave and developing a sort of friendship was one thing. Best not to get too entangled, though.

Caden didn't say anything. He merely went to the bathroom. Rushing water told Tate that the boy was washing up. When he returned with a soapy cloth, his pubic hair glistened and his cock was shiny clean. He washed Tate's finger and dick before tucking him under the sheet once more. Before he could go back to the bathroom, Tate grabbed his hand.

Caden looked at him from over his shoulder with a wary and shuttered expression. Tate couldn't blame him. He'd been running hot and cold with the boy since the beginning.

"Let's call a truce. We both wish our lives were different right now, but as that can't be, we should make the best of it."

Caden nodded with a slight smile. "That sounds good."

Tate gave his hand a squeeze before letting it go. "You'd best get dressed and I'll take a pain pill, please."

What the hell. His various injuries were screaming in fury. There was no point in fighting the relief. And as Caden pointed out, he was safe. There'd be opportunity enough to push for his recovery in order to make his escape. For the first time, though, he wondered about what would happen to Caden when he did. It was too much to think about, and given the slow rate of his recovery, it would be many weeks before that happened. No reason to worry about it. No reason at all.

* * * *

Tate lay drooling onto his pillow, fast asleep and looking more relaxed than Caden had seen him so far. Good sex and Vicodin would do that for you. And it *had* been good sex. There was no denying the fact, much as Caden might wish otherwise. Far from merely servicing the guy, they'd joined in a way that overrode their unequal status with each catering to the needs of the other. His bitchy young master's fingering had set him off like a rocket. For a few glorious seconds, he'd been liberated from his troubles, both his mind and body overtaken by intense pleasure.

God, as he sat curled in his usual chair by the window, he could still feel Tate's finger in his ass, somehow claiming him as much as being impaled on the man's cock would have. He'd known just how to coax arousal out of him, pushing that magic button inside as if he'd installed it there himself. Then the demand for Caden to jerk them both off had been both surprising and totally hot. The feel of grinding the hard shafts against one another had overridden memories of more interesting types of sex he'd been treated to in the past. Young he may be, but Tate Graham proved that inventiveness didn't need complexity or the experience of age. Caden felt both satisfied and eager for more.

Moreover, Tate had been kind to him afterward, as if coming together had stripped away the wall of antagonism that had consumed their interactions since his arrival. It hadn't quite equalized them, but it had proved that they had more in common than not. Each of them was imprisoned in their own way, unhappy with their fates and mad at the world. Of course, Tate had the extra luxury of using Caden as his whipping boy. The fact that he had called a truce and even offered an olive branch of friendship showed that the Tate of the last day wasn't the real one. Circumstances, confinement and pain had brought out the worst in the guy. And he might still revert to the bitter, angry man when he woke again. Caden was prepared for that, although he dared to hope that wasn't the case.

A noise, something raw and terrified, caught his attention. Over on the bed, Tate was becoming agitated. His head jerked back and forth, while his face contorted in fright.

A nightmare?

Figuring Tate was being plagued by memories of his crash, Caden put his book aside and went to…soothe the man, he supposed. It hadn't been more than a couple of hours since he'd taken the pain meds, so there was no help from that quarter. Maybe it would be best to wake him.

Tate began muttering, incoherently at first. Then, "Jimmy? Where the fuck are you? Come back! You're a swimmer. Why aren't you swimming?"

Caden stood by the side of the bed, hand raised, yet unsure if he should try to wake up Tate.

"Please, don't leave me."

It was that desperate plea, uttered in a small voice laced with heartbreaking fear and misery, that made the choice for him.

Caden laid his hand on his master's shoulder. "Tate." He shook him a little. "Tate, wake up. You're having a nightmare." He moved his hand to the man's head and tried again. "Everything's fine. You can wake up now."

Tate stilled. Then his eyes flew open, wild and unseeing. His chest heaved with sobbing breaths.

Unsure of what to do, Caden kept his hand where it was, but also stroked his thumb along Tate's forehead. "It's okay."

Tate's gaze shifted to him with clarity and focus now. "No, it's not okay. It's never going to be again."

Despite the warning blaring in his head to keep quiet, play the docile slave and mind his own business, he simply couldn't stay silent in the face of such misery. "Yes, it will. You're healing and will be out of this bed soon. Your life will go back to normal in a few months."

Tate barked out a mirthless laugh. "You think it's just this accident? My life was fucked well before I ran into that tree."

As he didn't have any response to that declaration, Caden simply stayed silent, stroking his master's forehead.

Tate hummed and his eyelids drooped. "That feels nice. My nanny used to do that to me whenever I had a nightmare."

"Not your mother?"

Tate snorted. "Seriously? You've met her. She's not exactly the maternal type."

Conjuring up his own memory of the woman made him shudder. "I guess not. At least you had a nice nanny," he couldn't help remarking, because his own childhood hadn't been filled with any kind of warmth.

"Yeah, I got lucky there, I suppose." He hesitated before adding, "And my brother. Jimmy was always there for me. Until he wasn't."

The words tearing out of Tate during the nightmare suddenly made sense. Some bit of news jogged his memory. The Grahams had two sons. One had died…somehow.

"He had a worse accident." Caden said the words out loud, the information flashing in his mind before he could censor himself. He stilled his thumb and held his breath. He'd gone too far in his presumptions that they were equals and capable of having a frank conversation.

Tate confirmed his concern by going utterly still, frigid in his expression and his body rigid. Then, instead of berating him and telling him to mind his own fucking business, Tate relaxed on a whoosh of air.

He turned to Caden. "We had one together. An accident, I mean. You think my skiing into a tree was stupid? Try going out on a small sailboat on Lake Michigan even though the weather report warned about possible squalls."

He looked away and stared up at the ceiling. "I knew I was taking a risk going down that difficult ski trail. Hell, I went to that resort specifically because of it. I confronted the danger and dared it to hurt me. It wasn't like being at the lake where you could look out over the water at sunshine and figured the weather would hold just because you couldn't see the trouble coming."

Tate pounded the bed with his free hand. "I knew better. We both did. Stupid. Stupid. I was always the cautious one and Jimmy the risk-taker. I should have insisted we not go."

Because Tate obviously needed the comfort, Caden used all his fingers to pet him and dared to place his other hand over Tate's. He braced for rejection. Instead, Tate turned his hand to lace their fingers.

"Who was older?" Again, he expected to be rebuked for asking.

"Jimmy." Tate's tone sounded a note of defeat, as if bringing up the accident drained him of confidence.

"So…he was sort of in charge, right? How could you have controlled what happened?"

"I couldn't. Jimmy always bowled me over in everything. And he was always right, too, so what did I know?"

Caden swept his gaze over the man's body, taking in the damage he was recovering from. Lots of people died from skiing accidents. Tate was both lucky and tough to have come out of his accident alive and relatively unscathed. "I guess you knew how to survive."

"Yeah right." Tate blinked up at him. "It was dumb luck. The squall capsized our boat before we could tack back to shore. We both got tossed out but I ended up closer to the upside-down hull. I managed to grab onto it. I looked around for Jimmy and called to him. I never saw or heard him. The water swallowed him up that fast, even though he was on the swim team."

Caden squeezed his hand briefly. "I guess swimming in a pool is much different than fighting waves in open water."

Tate let out an agonized grunt. "He would never wear a life jacket, said they were for people who couldn't swim as well as he could. Made fun of me for doing so," he added in a low voice. "I guess I was right about that, too."

"It might not have mattered. Maybe he hit his head before going in." Caden shrugged. "I don't suppose that's any comfort."

Tate squeezed his hand back. "No, see, it is because it validates my own thinking about it. I've told myself those things and I've mostly chased away survivor's guilt. I couldn't save Jimmy. Maybe if I'd seen him, I'd have let go of the boat to try to get him…but I didn't. So I held on until help came."

They fell silent for a while until Tate started coughing. Caden reluctantly let go of him, strangely liking the contact. He held a cup of water to Tate's lips, then helped him sit up, fluffing his pillows and making sure the sling and leg brace were placed properly. He brought his usual chair over to sit beside the bed but didn't try to initiate any more physical contact. The urgency from the nightmare had passed, leaving the gap in their positions a chance to reassert itself. Still, the sweet ache that came from sitting also reminded him of the intimacy they'd shared earlier. If nothing else, he wanted to experience that again, and perhaps it was okay to connect on a personal level that didn't involve sex.

He decided to push the concept. "May I ask you a question?"

Tate shrugged. "Sure."

"After losing your brother like that, why do you take such risks skiing?" He swept his gaze up and down Tate. "Maybe your brother's death was avoidable. Maybe not. This crash of yours was."

Tate rolled his eyes. "Oh, you're giving me too much credit if you think skiing black diamond runs is the only dangerous thing I do. I'm also into car and dirt bike racing. Base jumping. Rock climbing. Free soloing, too. I'm actually booked to summit Everest next year."

"I know. I've seen stories about your…exploits," Caden admitted, a little embarrassed that he'd read any gossip about his master.

"Oh yeah? Well, the things I do make me newsworthy." Tate seemed somewhat pleased by the idea. He sighed. "I guess I'll have to put all that stuff off until I'm back in shape."

"Or maybe not do it at all?" Caden ventured to suggest.

Tate chuckled. "Not an option. It's a challenge and it's risky. That put it on my to-try list. About the only thing I don't do anymore is anything that has to do with water." He closed his eyes briefly. "No more sailing or water skiing or jet skiing. The water is where Jimmy died. When I go, it's going to be on land or in the air."

Caden smacked his palm against his forehead. "Jesus! Why do you have to do something crazy and die young? You can't think that's what your brother would want."

Tate didn't answer for so long that Caden figured he wouldn't at all.

Finally, he got the rest of his story out, blinking back tears before he did. "No, Jimmy wouldn't like it but he'd understand why. It's my 'fuck you' to them. Our parents," he clarified, although it was pretty obvious whom he was referring to.

"You want them to lose their remaining son? I know they're pretty…"

"Horrid."

"Um, yeah."

Tate turned narrowed eyes on him. "Did my father fuck you before sending you here?"

"No!" The sudden question shocked him, and he didn't add that he was sure the man had wanted to. There was no point in riling Tate up even more than he was. "I'm for you. Only you."

Tate seemed to relax a bit with that answer. "Good. That would really piss me off for some reason. And I'm not risking their son. I'm risking their heir."

"I don't understand the difference." Except he kind of did. The Grahams had a dynasty to pass on to the next generation as a way of immortalizing themselves.

"It was supposed to be Jimmy. God, how they doted on him. He was everything they wanted in a child. I was simply insurance. You know, as if we were royalty or something. Always have to have a spare lying around, just in case."

"That doesn't mean they didn't want you or...love you." From the little he'd seen of Tate's parents, he didn't think that kind of soft emotion was something they were capable of. He hoped he was wrong, but...

Tate shook his head slowly. "God, you're naïve in your own way. They don't love me. Never have. I don't think they loved Jimmy, either, but he was exactly what they wanted so that made them happy with him. When I was sitting in the back of the ambulance after they fished me out and were still searching for Jimmy, my parents drove up. The looks on their faces as they raced over and saw me confirmed what I always had known."

Caden's stomach clenched, waiting for what he knew was coming.

"Disappointment. Crushingly so. They'd been told one of their sons had been rescued. They had expected...*hoped* it was Jimmy. At least, that's what I figured as they stared at me. They've never said as much. They didn't have to. I knew."

"I'm sorry." It was all he could think to say because, Jesus. It was movie-level drama. It made him almost glad to be an only child. At least his father's indifference hadn't been outright dislike. He'd been an annoyance to the man, not a disappointment.

"Don't be. There's something liberating about knowing I don't have anyone else to worry about. If I die, no one will mourn me."

"Seems to me like you're hoping you will bite it just to spite them."

"You've got that right. My dying would have the added benefit of pissing them off, because then they would have no one to carry on the family name and legend in business. The ultimate pay-back for their not wanting me." He sighed. "Of course, they'd probably buy a surrogate slave and give it another try using at least Dad's genes. God, poor kid."

"This all seems like an extreme way to distance yourself from them. You don't have to die to give them the finger. Why not simply disown them instead? Take away their heir without ending up buried six feet under."

Tate tossed his head. "Because I'm a spoiled asshole. I have a decent inheritance from my grandmother, but if I leave my parents, I'm giving up *billions*. If nothing else, their money allows me to fund my sports."

"And if you die from your fun, you can't take the money with you, so other than giving your parents a big 'fuck you', what is your goal here?"

"I don't really have one, I guess. It's just that at the moment before I start something dangerous, like skiing down that slope, I feel alive. Really alive, the way I used to before the accident. And the rush I get while doing it shuts out every bad thought and memory I have. For a few minutes, I'm free of everything. So, yeah, I don't really have a goal beyond screwing with my parents and those few minutes." He shot Caden a grin. "But now, maybe it's playing with your ass again. How is it, by the way?"

Okay, if his master wanted to change the subject, he had no choice. "Hungry for your dick instead of your finger. Better heal up fast." He gave the man a coquettish grin, marveling that he both wanted and dared to after their rocky start.

Tate gave him a smoldering look in return. "That's a pretty good incentive." His grin turned into a frown. "How did you end up becoming a debt slave?"

Despite Tate's soul-bearing, Caden found it hard to reciprocate. He dropped his gaze. "The usual way. I have too much debt to pay any other way. My creditors were starting to cry fraud, too, in order to get paid, so I was worried about going to prison."

"That's crazy at your age. What, are you a compulsive gambler or something because you were obviously raised in at least the middle class? You must have had some money and opportunities. Was there some kind of family debt you had to take care of? Come on. I spilled my guts. You do the same."

"All right." Caden took a deep breath. "It's not a very interesting story. You're right about my upbringing. I had all the right advantages as a kid, but didn't take going to college seriously. Dropped out after one semester. Partied a lot. Then I met and fell in love with an older man who sucked me dry and put me deep in debt without my realizing it. He kept me well-fucked and dazzled with his charm. Before the creditors came knocking at my door, he'd left me weeping and wondering what I'd done wrong and where my inheritance had gone." He shrugged. "Not billions, but I would have been set for life if I'd been relatively careful. And if I hadn't blown off my education, I would probably be on my way to having a lucrative profession to either add to the nice nest egg my lucky birth had provided, or to dig myself out of the hole my asshole lover dropped me into. I didn't, so here I am, wiping your ass and jerking you off." He grinned to soften his harsh words. "Not that I'm complaining… too much."

Instead of taking offense and issuing a rebuke, Tate held out his hand and smiled when Caden took it. "What a pair we are. Still, we're stuck with our mistakes and marooned in paradise. If we hold on to each other, we'll be okay."

Caden wasn't sure that was true. Tate certainly would be. His own fate was uncertain. And yet, for this moment, with Tate's hand warmly clasping his, he could allow himself to feel at least a little happy.

Chapter Five

"I don't think this is a very good idea. It's too soon."

Tate shot Caden a glare and tried harder to hide his pain. "Well, good thing I'm the master, huh, and it's my decision? I'm plenty ready to get out of this damn bed and feel the sun on my face for a while."

His words were a little ridiculous given that it had taken two burly groundskeepers to lift him off the bed and set him in the wheelchair he insisted Miss Ophelia have delivered. It was stuffed with a pillow for his back and shoulders, a head rest for when holding his up became too tiring, and a horizontal brace for his leg. It was not, he noted, electric. Obviously, the intent was to make him dependent on being pushed around instead of giving him the autonomy to make his own way. It was both a ploy to keep him under control and to prevent him from doing something risky, like careening down some stairs and maybe putting himself into a full body cast. *Or break my neck this time.* Still, he was somewhere other than in bed and he'd take the win.

Once he was settled, he looked around at the people hovering as if he were some ancient man trying to enjoy the last of his remaining days. The nurse in particular was staring at him with pursed lips, livid that her judgment had been overridden. She'd been no more persuasive than Caden had on this topic and because he wasn't having sex with her, he'd ignored her opinion entirely. With Caden, he'd at least listened to the pleas with some amount of patience. He liked the guy, plain and simple, and despite it making no sense given that the slave had been sent by his parents, he believed Caden genuinely worried about him. He still wasn't going to let go of the idea of getting outside. And Caden would be there to both help him and take his orders. That was something, at least.

"See? I'm fine." He turned to Caden. "I'm making you the designated driver. Let's go onto the patio."

"Okay, whatever you say."

Caden first laid a cotton blanket across his lap for modesty's sake. Tate continued to wear only hospital smocks in deference to his injuries and nothing else. His ass and junk were mostly covered, but not by much. There was a lot of naked thigh showing, which apparently bothered Caden more than it did him. It was kind of cute the way his slave tucked the covering around him. He had to focus on Nurse Ratched's pinched face to keep himself from responding in a way that would have proved far more embarrassing to all of them.

Caden quirked his lips, as if he knew what effect he had on him, then moved behind the wheelchair to take hold of the handles. Unlocking the brakes, the boy pushed him tentatively toward the door. Everyone else stood watching, mentally wringing their hands no doubt. They needn't have worried. Caden was taking great care to maneuver the wheelchair so as not to bump anything. The slow pace was fine with Tate. He wasn't a masochist keen on becoming a human pinball, and it was forward movement. That was what mattered. The people in the room parted like the Red Sea at his approach. Soon, he was in his sitting room, a place he had only spied through the open door for weeks. Not that it held his interest. He wanted to be outside, taking advantage of the benefit of being cooped up on a tropical island. It was a little pathetic how much he was looking forward to it.

The path was clear, no servants stood around watching the show, and those that had been in the bedroom hurried past him when he waved for them to do so. He didn't want or need an audience and now that Caden had demonstrated his navigation skills, they no longer had a reason to stick around. A short trip down the hall and he was at the elevator. Caden maneuvered around the awkward space to back the chair in and send them to the first floor. The French doors leading to one of the patios dotted around the house was right across from them when they arrived. Some smart person had already opened them. All the slave needed to do was push him in a straight line.

"Put me over there by the railing."

Caden complied, braking the chair as near as he could get without bumping Tate's foot into the wrought iron barrier.

Tate closed his eyes and tipped his head back to soak up the sunlight. He sighed. "It's embarrassing how wonderful this feels. Almost as good as fingering you."

Caden snorted at the confession. "I expect even small pleasures become larger after being confined to bed. You can finger me while sunbathing if you want, of course."

Despite the teasing tone, Tate took the words seriously.

He opened his eyes and found Caden leaning against the railing with his hands braced on it. The guy was wearing board shorts and a T-shirt, so no part of his body was easily accessible. Not that Tate would even try to touch him intimately out in the open like this. He had some standards, after all.

"There are too many people around who might see. I wouldn't expose you to others like that."

Caden lowered his gaze. "I appreciate the consideration, but I did sign up for anything. My feelings aren't important."

"Bullshit!" Tate found himself getting mad on the boy's behalf. "*I* didn't sign a damn thing, and how you feel about something matters to me. Unlike my parents, I'm not an asshole. Not much, anyway," he amended, remembering how he'd treated Caden when he'd first arrived.

Caden gave him a little smile. "You're not an asshole at all. I understand you're in pain and upset about effectively being held a prisoner by your parents." He looked at the garden behind him. "Not having control over your life is hard even if you're stuck in paradise."

Tate shifted his sling, ignoring the twinge of pain as he did so. "It's not forever. A few more weeks maybe. The doctor is coming on Thursday to take out my stitches and hopefully put me in a walking cast. I was in top physical condition before the accident. It won't take much time for me to get back into shape. Then we're out of here."

Caden turned to grip the railing and stared at the garden beyond it intently. "I wonder how long it will be before you hurt yourself again and maybe end up right back here. Or worse."

The remark would have stung if not for the worry he heard in the guy's tone.

"I always get dinged up. This was unusually bad. I usually don't end up in the hospital, doped to the gills and an easy target for my parents' control. Besides, if I do get hurt again, you'll be there to nurse me back to health like you are now." It surprised him how much he liked the idea of Caden staying by his side.

"Will I?"

The question surprised him. "Of course. My parents bought you for me. Where else would you be?"

Caden shrugged but didn't look at him. "I don't know. They want me to keep you occupied while you're here. Once you're back on your feet and living your life again, I won't be useful anymore. They'll sell me to someone else, I guess."

The very idea made Tate so mad, he reared up in the wheelchair. Pain shot through damn well everywhere. "Fuck!"

Alarmed, Caden shot over to him. "Easy now. Sit back."

Tate did as he was told but grabbed the boy's hand when he tried to move away again. "I won't let them do that."

Caden smiled briefly. "Okay."

"You don't believe me?"

"I think your parents are very controlling people and see me as a means to a short-term end. They hold my contract, not you."

Tate was on the verge of promising to buy the contract from them and making Caden his own. The words stuck in his throat, however. Who was he to own anyone and really, what made him think Caden wanted to stay with him? Sure, the sex was great, but they were young. It was easy to enjoy sex with someone in any circumstances. Their dicks weren't exactly picky. Caden had said he was attracted to older men. He might really like being with a contemporary of his parents more than being with him.

Of course he could buy the contract and set Caden free. He had the money to spare, and that would leave Caden free to do whatever he wanted with the rest of his life before a full ten fucking years of his life went by. His parents would have to agree to sell the boy to him, and probably wouldn't out of spite and a pathological need to always be on top, win at everything with everyone. On the other hand, so what if they refused? The law had one sort of good loophole in that any slave could break the contract if they wanted to end up right back in the same debt with the added penalty of a break-up fee. Who ever did that? Owing even more than you could pay off with a normal amount of work was hardly a viable choice for those slaves. Then again, he could pay it on Caden's behalf. He liked the idea of doing that for him, although he wasn't sure Caden would agree to it. The guy had pride. Knowing that kind of made Tate mad. He liked to be in control, too, apparently. And really, he barely knew the slave. Becoming his savior was a little crazy.

Throttling back his emotions, Tate let go of Caden's hand. "That's all a ways' off still. We can figure it out later. Let's take a walk through the gardens." This patio had stairs on only one side. The other sloped down into the gardens via a crushed shell path, joining a maze of them that wound through the lush bushes and plants.

Caden appeared dubious about that idea. "Really? The walkway is pretty narrow and bumpy with those shell pieces. No matter how slow I go, you're going to be jostled."

"I don't care. Any discomfort it causes me is worth it."

"Whatever you say, Master." Caden released the brakes.

Tate held on to the armrest with his one free hand as the wheelchair got rolling. "Were you trying to bait me, calling me that?"

Caden chuckled. "Yes, did it work?"

"Yes," Tate ground out. "Why risk my wrath? Slaves are supposed to be respectful and obedient." Now, it was his turn to do the teasing.

Caden didn't answer right away and when he did, it was surprisingly poignant. "I suppose because I feel…safe with you."

Tate's heart tripped a little with unexpected emotion. "You are. I promise." Even as he said it, he knew that wasn't entirely true. While he wasn't going to hurt the boy, he couldn't control how anyone else might treat him. Not in his present condition. He needed to get better and stronger. Then he could protect them both.

"Take this left path. I want to see the fountain at the end of it."

Caden steered him in that direction, going maddeningly slowly. It was for Tate's own good, he understood that. Still, he'd been inactive for so long, he wanted to feel the rush of speed even if it was while under the power of something other than himself. Not wanting to bother Caden by making him do something he wasn't comfortable with, he forced himself to relax and enjoy the sights along the way. The grounds really were exquisite, filled with colorful native plants that gave it a natural look even though it was ruthlessly groomed. He supposed the garden was like everything else in his parents' lives — effortlessly completely controlled without obvious oppression, unless one knew where and how to look and analyze the details.

The fountain coming into view eased his agitation. He'd always loved it as a child because of the wanton fantasy of it. His parents' tastes usually ran to more sophisticated and understated décor. Three sirens carved out of marble, bare-breasted, and with curvaceous, seductive smiles surrounded a thin column of the same stone, out of the top of which the water spouted. Despite knowing he was gay from an early age, he'd still found those women impossibly mesmerizing. Erotically enticing, as well, although he didn't understand his reaction as such until puberty had hit. He imagined joining them under the sea where he fantasized they went every night, thinking it as a great escape from real life.

Caden parked him beside it. "Is this what you're looking for?"

"Mmm. Yeah. I can stare at them for hours. Jimmy and both used to as kids, actually. By the time we were twelve, he dared to touch their nipples when no one was looking. I think he might have jerked off to visions of them when he went to bed." His brother had loved girls, then women, the hot and sexy kind, even when they were made of marble.

Caden snorted. "A straight boy, huh? Well, this would do it, I suppose. Not you, though, right?"

Tate shook his head. "Obviously not. I found them alluring in the sense that they represented a fantasy world that I longed for."

Caden cocked his head as he stared at the statues. "I can see that. Sirens live under the sea, then come up to lure men to their deaths. But I bet you were thinking more of *The Little Mermaid*, a world of color and fun and a tight family. Better than what you had up here."

A warmth spread through Tate at hearing how well Caden got him. They made a good couple if he thought about it. Not that he should. He was getting ahead of himself again. "You hit my fantasy right on the head. I figured they couldn't find me twenty thousand leagues under the sea. How about you? Ever dream of escaping boarding school?"

A wistful look came over the slave's face. "When I was younger, sure. I used to imagine that my mother wasn't dead and she'd pull up one day and take me home." He shrugged. "That didn't last long. Once I realized I was surrounded by hot guys in a dark room, I didn't mind being there."

Tate took the cue and changed the tone of the conversation. "Lot of groping, huh, after lights out."

"Oh yes. Even the straight boys were happy to have a hand job. Or a blow job when we got older. The teachers liked it too."

Tate made a face. "Ew. Isn't that illegal and shit, immoral?"

"I'm sure it's both, but remember how I said I liked older men."

Tate wondered if that preference was a direct result of the predatory behavior of those teachers, but that was too heavy a topic. He went back to staring at the fountain. "Anyway, I never jerked off to these three

lovelies. Now, if this were a fountain of Poseidon..."
He wiggled his eyebrows and grinned.

Caden laughed. "Oh yeah. A big, powerful man.
That would do it for me, too." He narrowed his gaze. "I
don't have that god's physique, but..."

Before Tate realized the boy's intent, Caden stripped
off his T-shirt, toed out from his sneakers and wiggled
his shorts down. He was left wearing his thong
underwear. Tate was so distracted by the sudden sight
of the creamy ass, he missed Caden's intent until he'd
already climbed into the fountain.

Caden let out a short shriek. "God, it's colder than I
would have expected. I thought tropical water is
supposed to be warm."

Tate chuckled. "It is in the ocean. This water is
pumped from the ground. You're going to shrivel your
balls off if you don't get out."

The slave ignored his warning and waded through
the water until he stood beside the statue. Then he
struck a pose, flashing his naked ass in Tate's direction
and giving him a sultry look over his shoulder.

"What do you think, Master? Would I make a good
siren?"

"You know damn well you would and do, you little
tease." He gestured to where his blanket tented from
his suddenly hard cock.

With no one around, it had free rein to give into the
temptation. He wanted so much for Caden to put his
hand or mouth on him and ease his ache. In his aroused
state, his brain and his dick were on the same page. He
couldn't have cared less about being seen.

"Come here."

The coquettish look on Caden's face morphed into
one of hunger. That was the only way to describe it.

And his tiny thong did nothing to hide his erection, either. Knowing that the slave who served him wanted the sex as much as he did was even more of a turn on.

Caden splashed his way over and climbed out of the fountain. Instead of dropping to his knees beside the wheelchair, he released the brakes and pushed Tate past the fountain and down a path that led to a small bench. Tate opened his mouth to object, then saw what the boy had in mind. This little alcove provided some amount of privacy, plus offered Caden a comfortable place to settle.

He parked the chair beside the bench and sat down. "What do you want?"

The boy's beauty, bathed in spots of sun shining through the leaves, left Tate's mouth dry. He had to swallow to speak. "Anything you're willing to give."

"I'd love to suck you off, but the chair makes it awkward. We'll have to settle for my hand."

Tate was on the verge of telling him that being jerked off wasn't *settling*. He lost the power of speech as soon as Caden slid his hand under the blanket and past the hem of Tate's smock to clasp his cock.

"Huh," was all he was able to say.

Caden surprised and disappointed him by taking his own cock out. "You don't mind if I take care of us both at the same time, do you?"

Tate wanted to say yes, he did, that he wanted the pleasure of jerking the boy off himself.

Instead, all he could do was grunt and stare as Caden worked both their shafts in synced rhythm. The garden was filled with birdsong, the buzz of insects and their harsh breathing as their climaxes built in tandem. Heat from more than the sunny, humid weather wrapped around him. He focused his gaze on the tip of the slave's dick, at the pre-cum already making it shiny, and the way it disappeared for a moment inside the cup of its owner's fingers before peeping out again. When ropes of cum pulsed out of it, he gave into his own orgasm.

For long seconds, he lost his senses completely, not seeing or hearing anything. It was that oblivion, that little death as it was called, that came from a strong release that allowed him to forget...everything. Here, there was no pain, not physical or emotional, his brother wasn't dead and his parents weren't the enemy. There was merely bliss. He came back slowly, panting as if he'd run a marathon. He hated the weakness of his body, but he couldn't resent it too much. It had brought him Caden, and these mounting moments of peace and pleasure.

The boy sat back, his cheeks blooming in a pretty pink, and held up his hands. "I've made a mess." Then he wiped them on his chest, leaving a trail of milky cum from both their bodies glistening on his smooth chest.

"You little tease. It's like waving a crust of bread in front of a starving man who can't take a bite."

Caden tipped his chin. "Would you like to bite me?"

"Come here and I'll show you how much." Tate practically growled at the idea.

"Um, no. Sorry, it would overtask you. I'll just go wash up in the fountain and get dressed again. It's not like people drink from it, right?"

Tate didn't answer, but he did twist around to watch Caden's gleaming white ass as he sauntered away. His collarbone screamed at him. He told it to shut the fuck up. Caden was a vision worth any pain. And as the boy splashed water on himself, he looked like something otherworldly. Not a siren, yet something that could be just as deadly if Tate weren't careful.

* * * *

"There, that's the last of them."

Caden hovered as the doctor removed the final stitch from Tate's leg. The scars from both breaks were ugly and Tate was obviously still stiff and in some amount of pain. This was progress at least, a sign that Tate was heading toward full healing. And that would mean leaving the island. For both of them. He hated the thought of it. No matter what Tate said, Caden was certain the Grahams were going to pass him along to another master once their son was fit to defy them again.

And what had they accomplished by sending him here? Sure, he was a distraction for Tate, a friendly helper who came with the added benefit of great sex. They hadn't needed him to keep Tate on the island, however. His injuries and the army of servants loyal to his parents had seen to that. At most, Caden had merely kept him from hounding them about his confinement. He couldn't even get Tate to look at any of the endless business documents that Miss Ophelia printed out and handed to him. Tate simply threw them all away without so much as a glance. If there was a grander, more complex plan in all of this, he couldn't see it. Any day now, he expected to be told to get back on that plane and shuttled off to someone else, a failure in the Grahams' schemes.

There was no point in dwelling on his future. He should be happy enough that his time with Tate was proving to be enjoyable. It was more than he could have hoped for or expected, especially after the first few days. Something had changed between them since then. It was friendship, he supposed, with benefits. It couldn't ever be anything more than that, no matter what Tate had raised as a possible life together. Not that the guy had specifically said he wanted that or anything. He'd merely talked in terms of taking Caden away from his parents' control. It sounded like a great idea, in a vague fantasy kind of way. If he allowed himself, Caden could imagine staying with Tate, warming his bed and keeping him company while he went back to taking stupid risks with dangerous sports. He didn't think he could deal with that kind of stress and it would probably hurt when Tate inevitably hooked up with other men. Free men.

The doctor stuck a jar in front of his face, forcing him out of his head. "Here's some cream. Rub it into his scars to help them stay supple and heal."

Caden took it. "Yes, sir."

"Oh, a little light massage from my slave. Sounds like fun." Tate grinned at the doctor.

Caden had to work to keep from rolling his eyes. He put the cream on the nightstand, intending to use it once they were alone. Tate's reaction to his touch was easily anticipated. As was his own. There was no way he'd do that in front of everyone else.

The doctor merely grunted and packed up his bag. "Come with me, boy. I need to talk to you."

It took Caden a moment to realize the man was addressing him. "Oh, um." He looked at Tate.

"What do you want him for?"

"Just a few more instructions from your parents. Nothing you need to concern yourself with, Mr. Graham. Get some rest."

Before Tate could object, the doctor grabbed Caden by the arm and forced him toward the door.

"Hey!" Tate's voice was angry.

But there was nothing for either of them to do. The doctor shut the door after him and propelled Caden over to the sofa in Tate's sitting room. They were alone, and the moment the man's ass hit the cushion, Caden could tell what he wanted.

"Suck me off."

Caden blinked at him, hesitating, because he didn't know what he should do. He was there for Tate, yet wasn't his slave. He knew he didn't have the right to object to anything and wasn't sure Tate did, either.

"Mrs. Graham told me to make use of you while I was here. She knows it takes up my whole day to come, and is generous in giving me an added bonus." The man's affable demeanor had turned into meanness.

Well, that settled that. Caden had to do as his owners commanded. That was the deal, and he literally couldn't afford to disobey.

The doctor patted his crotch. "Now, slut!"

Hiding his resentment as best he could, Caden dropped to his knees between the man's spread legs. He reached for his belt.

"Stop!"

The order startled both him and the doctor. They looked over to see Tate standing in the doorway, grimacing, and bracing himself against the jamb with obvious difficulty.

"Tate, you shouldn't be out of bed on your own." Caden rose to go over to him.

The doctor grabbed his arm and kept him from doing so. "Your slut's right. Go back and lie down. We can't have you falling and injuring something else. I'll have him back to you soon enough."

"Get your fucking hands off him. Caden, come here."

Tate's commanding tone gave Caden permission to yank free of the doctor's hand. He raced over to slip Tate's arm around his shoulder. The guy sagged with obvious relief, but he trembled, too, whether from anger or physical weakness, he couldn't tell.

The doctor huffed to his feet. "Your mother gave me permission to use him."

"Tough shit. Get out and find something else to stick your dick into, like a couch cushion. Caden is mine."

The declaration thrilled him a bit, even if it was probably based on possessiveness and not genuine affection or concern.

"Your parents will hear of this. He's a slave, not a boyfriend."

"Feel free to tell them that I wasn't willing to share my fuck toy with you. I want to keep him unsoiled for my use only. I should think they'd appreciate that sentiment. Now, get out of my sight."

Tate didn't wait for the doctor to move. Instead, he turned, leaning even more heavily on Caden, and made his way back to bed. Caden helped him sit on the edge. Tate landed on his back with a groan, half in, half out.

Caden helped get him fully on, grimacing at the guy's low moan as he moved his injured leg, then tucked him under the sheet. It was strange not to see all of the contraptions that he'd been hooked up to anymore. The moaning and how white and sweaty the man's skin was from the short trip to the doorway and back made it clear he was still recovering.

"You shouldn't have gotten out of bed and walked on your own. It's too early for that. And the doctor was right. You could have fallen down and hit your head." He glared at Tate. "Then there would we be?"

Tate's expression hardened. "I knew what that asshole was up to when he dragged you out of here. I wasn't going to let him exploit you. And not because I thought it would make you dirty. It's just... Well, you didn't sign up to be manhandled by anyone who demands it."

Touched, Caden sat gingerly on the side of the bed. "I kind of did, actually. Giving the doctor a blow job would have been no big deal. Certainly not worth your risking yourself over."

"It should be!" Tate softened his expression immediately. "Sorry, I don't mean to take my anger out on you. And who am I to talk, given how I use you?"

It was weird to be in the role of comforter, but that's what Caden decided he needed to be at the moment. "It's not the same. I like giving you a blow job or hand job. It's fun. So that makes it all right."

"Does it?" Tate scrunched up his face. "I don't think so. This situation is starting to feel really wrong. I mean, it always did feel that way but at first, I was too wrapped up in my own pain and misery to give it much scrutiny. I'm sorry about that."

Standing, Caden reached for the jar of cream. "You have nothing to apologize for. And there's nothing either of us can do about it. Railing against the injustice of my being a slave isn't going to help either of us." He held up the jar. "Do you want me to rub this into your incisions?"

"Do you want me to get hard?"

"Yes." That was the bald truth.

"Then, yes. Please." With a sigh, Tate lay back against his pillows. "He's going to report all of this to my parents."

Caden scooped out a finger full of cream and sniffed it. Lavender. *Nice*. "Sure he will. So what?"

Untying the back of Tate's smock, he lowered the front to expose the man's chest. Even after a few weeks in bed, Tate was jacked. Drooling over his hard pecs was better than focusing on the ugly scar slashing across it from the surgery. He figured starting with Tate's collarbone was the safest course of action. Rubbing the cream into the leg last would have the obvious effect and lead to the place they both wanted him to go.

Tate stared at the ceiling and shook his head. "I don't know. My parents are always a problem. I'm not ready to leave under my own power yet, but they might decide I don't need you anymore. Or more to the point, believe they've lost control over you so you're no longer useful to them. Worse, you might have turned into my ally. They can't have that."

Tate had hit the nail on the head. Whatever loyalty a slave might have to the ones who owned them, his had definitely landed with Tate. He couldn't imagine not doing what this man wanted and needed. He was developing emotions, too, that were dangerous for someone in his position. The idea of being forced to leave Tate shot fear in him before he forced it away.

"There's nothing we can do about that, now is there? No point in fretting over what we can't control. Now, let's see how hard I can make you."

Chapter Six

"One more rep. Come on, don't be a baby."

Tate really didn't think he had it in him, but Caden did, and his slave's confidence gave him strength. Ignoring the sweat dripping into his eyes and the scream of his muscles, Tate raised the barbell one more time. He glared at Caden as he set the weights down. "Slavedriver."

Caden's eyes went wide. "Seriously? What is this, opposite week, *Master*?"

Tate reached for his towel and swatted it at the guy. Caden danced out of reach, testament to how one of them was in tip-top shape and the other, not so much. *I'm getting there.* With his limbs liberated from their restraints and his stitches removed, it was up to him to restrengthen his body. The physical therapist motored over from St. Thomas every few days to give him new exercises, but it was Caden who oversaw his daily efforts based on a schedule the PT provided. And the slave did his own exercise alongside him. Working out together made the whole thing more bearable. Watching the boy work up a sweat was a great incentive. He would have loved to have him do so in only a thong, but the floor to ceiling windows along one wall meant someone could see them and he didn't want to embarrass his slave like that. He had to be content with a sleeveless T-shirt and tight shorts to entice him.

And it did. After the gym, they showered together, jerking their cocks to mutual completion. It was hotter than most of his other sexual encounters, but also left him more worn out than it should. He always napped afterward, like a baby. It was frustrating, yet Caden was there when he woke to spend the rest of the day with. They'd taken to playing cards and board games, as well as watching TV. And he often creamed Tate, which he appreciated. He didn't want to be allowed to win. It also proved that Caden was smart as well as gorgeous. If he applied himself, there was nothing he couldn't do. It made his slave status that much more poignant. Ten years would be wasted before Caden would have the chance to make something of himself.

I can change that. I have the power to set him free.

The thought cheered him, although it was too soon for him to put any kind of plan in action. Still, he thought about it, more and more these days. There was time, though, and Caden was good company. It had been years since Tate had spent so much time with someone else outside of the bedroom. Not since…Jimmy.

Telling Caden about the accident that had cost him his brother and how damaged his feelings were afterward had been cleansing. A kind of therapy, something he'd dismissed out of hand when a doctor had recommended it. He'd always told people he was fine, right before heading off to another risky adventure. Somehow, Caden's quiet comfort had loosened his tongue and he didn't regret it. His resentment toward the boy had evaporated in the wake of his confession, not to mention the constant companionship that was developing into a real friendship. He was glad his parents had sent him the slave to keep him occupied. They wouldn't understand how personal things had become between them.

In their world, everything was transactional. Feelings, true ones, nice ones, weren't something he figured they could ever manage. And Caden was nothing more than a tool, something useful, and with the ability to spy on Tate on their behalf. That was a part of the boy's services that they never talked about, not really — only so much as to form a united front about how to manage that part of his job. The fact that Caden hadn't denied it had made their alliance on it something that Tate could believe and depend on. The first evening Miss Ophelia had come to take Caden away for a call, the boy had winked at Tate behind her back. When he'd returned, he'd reassured Tate that he'd given an account of a belligerent master who reluctantly accepted Caden's intimate services.

It was only your father and he wanted details. *I told him you used my mouth and hand at your convenience, showing a little resentment as I did. He reminded me to do my duty and keep you happy or he'd sell me off.*

Caden had shuddered in gest at the last bit. Tate didn't find it amusing, however. It had been a reminder that Caden belonged to his parents, not him. He hadn't really cared at the time. Now, it was different. Now, he *did* care. Too much, maybe, and in a way he wasn't entirely comfortable with. If he did nothing else, he had to be sure to maneuver them into setting the boy up in a good situation once they were off the island. The thought of Caden living the next nine and half years or so under the thumb of someone like his father made his blood run cold. The slave didn't deserve that fate. The idea of keeping him for himself popped into his head with more frequency. But no, nothing had changed for Tate. He couldn't offer Caden much of a life as a slave or a boyfriend. When he was fully recovered, he intended to continue as he had. His anger at his parents hadn't abated, and they for sure hadn't stopped trying to steer him into the life they demanded for him.

"Are you all right?"

Tate came back to himself, out of the dark recesses of his head and back to the gym where he sat with sweat cooling his skin. He glanced at Caden's concerned face. "I'm fine. Thanks. Just tired."

"Time for a nap, then." Caden held out his hand.

Tate took it and allowed the boy to haul him to his feet. A spurt of arousal egged him into a decision. His thoughts might have strayed to a future that was too far off to plan for but his immediate one was his to control any way he wanted.

Leaning in, he whispered into Caden's ear. "I'm going to fuck you tonight. Right into the mattress. Then we'll see who's driving whom tomorrow in here."

Caden shuddered and his breath quickened. "I guess we'd both better take a nap, then. After a shower." He gave Tate an enticing look.

His cock twitched, then slowly filled with blood, pressing against his shorts. "Careful. I'm still recovering. I might not be able to handle a hand job in the shower, then a good fuck tonight."

Caden's expression turned to one of concern. "Really? I'm sorry. I don't mean to overtax you."

With a laugh, Tate slung his arm over the boy's shoulders. "I'm only teasing. If you get to be too much for me, I'll let you know." He herded him out of the room, his dick leading the way.

* * * *

Miss Ophelia peered at Tate's empty plate. "Someone's finally got his appetite back."

Tate gave the woman a cocky smile. "Yes, ma'am. My slave makes sure I don't skimp on my PT. Leaves me hungry." He dared to shoot a look at Caden to send a different meaning.

Caden's blushed and dropped his gaze. "Just doing my duty, sir." He peeked up at him from under his lashes.

Tate's dick jumped. Good thing they were sitting at the table. Miss Ophelia undoubtedly got a full accounting from the laundress about the state of his sheets and knew what Caden's duties entailed. Still, he didn't want to embarrass the woman.

She snorted as she oversaw the removal of their dinner and swatted him lightly on his good shoulder as she left. There was no fooling her, and if she were reporting back to his parents, at least she could confirm that Caden was telling the truth when he said he was servicing him. Whether she detected their growing friendship—a thing his parents certainly did not intend—was hard to know. He had to hope she kept anything of the sort to herself, regardless. Everyone on the island was his jailor, but this was a woman who had always taken his side as best she could. He had to believe that she would continue to do so as much as she could for him without jeopardizing her position as house manager. It was easy to keep up the pretense about Caden being nothing more than a sex toy, really. There was nothing Caden could do to liberate Tate anyway. He wasn't a danger to his parents' plans. A friendship with benefits was going to help keep Tate docile more than anything, whether he wanted it to or not. The urge to escape had muted since he'd started enjoying the time he spent with his slave.

There were other compulsions that had risen once more, however, overriding everything else. He stood and beckoned the boy. "Come on."

Caden followed him back into the bedroom, quiet yet with a tension radiating off him that matched Tate's.

He was careful to shut and lock the door, as well as close the curtains. Caden had said he didn't think there was surveillance in the room after he'd spent time roaming around and looking. Tate wasn't convinced, but his incessant hard-on made him less concerned about being discreet. While the bathroom might be a safer place to fuck Caden, he wanted to use the bed. A real one had replaced the hospital contraption and it was plenty big enough for two.

He grabbed Caden by the arms, intending to drag him over to it. But he got caught up in the vivid green of the boy's eyes. This close he could see that the color reminded him of the ocean surrounding their luscious prison. He'd always loved staring at the sea and these eyes captivated him just as much. He fell into them, mesmerized. Then he did something he hadn't intended to do. He kissed him.

The way Caden's eyes widened just before their mouths touched revealed his surprise. It didn't matter. Nothing did after that first sweet taste of his lips. Not one for romantic foreplay, Tate nevertheless was hooked for more. His throbbing dick faded into the background as Tate explored Caden's mouth, first with his lips on the outside, then with his tongue inside. The boy yielded to him as he always did, with quiet obedience and a willingness to be led to pleasure.

Tate tugged the slave close, backing toward the bed while holding the kiss. Caden grabbed onto his waist and moaned as their dicks brushed against one another. When the backs of his legs hit the edge of the bed, Tate whirled around to tumble Caden onto the mattress. Someone had already turned down the sheets. Cool, crisp cotton stretched over a thick, tufted mattress, enveloped them.

The need for air forced Tate to pull back. Not far. Only as much as necessary for him to nibble along Caden's jaw. He roamed as much of the boy's body as he could reach with his hands. Every inch was smooth skin layered onto well-toned muscles. Caden was fit but not ripped. Tate appreciated the difference. He liked his boys to be a little delicate looking and feeling—a contrast to himself. And Caden smelled really good, a bit flowery without being girly. He inhaled deeply as he nuzzled the slave's neck. The scent shot straight to his dick, making it even harder, if such a thing were possible.

He bucked his hard cock along the matching ridge of Caden's shorts as he continued his assault with mouth and hands. They both groaned and shuddered. The intensity of it all threatened to make him come too soon. He was no longer satisfied with just getting off.

He wanted to bury himself deep into Caden's ass, be cocooned in the wet heat he knew he'd find there, before emptying his balls. The mere thought of it nearly sent him over the edge.

Tate slid off, pulling Caden to his feet. He yanked the dazed boy's T-shirt over his head, stopping only for a moment to kiss his puffy pink lips briefly. The shorts came next, freeing the dick that he was quickly learning and appreciating well. The slave was as aroused as he was. He wanted to pick him up and toss him back on the bed. A twinge from his shoulder warned him it was too soon.

"Lie on the bed." He issued the order without thought.

Caden didn't seem to mind. In fact, he grinned. "Yes, Master."

Tate paused in his own undressing to consider how he thought about that response. He liked it. A lot. In this context, at least. Here it was more like a game they could play without the outside world giving it a meaning neither of them liked.

Pulling off his shorts, he added, "On your back, legs spread, knees bent. I want to look at your pretty face when I fuck you."

Oh yeah, his cock pulsed as he issued his commands. He'd known he was born to take charge. The fact that Caden acted as if he liked playing the slave now even though he resented being one legally confirmed that he was on board with the game. The sex was going to be amazing.

Tate pumped some lotion onto both hands and coated his dick as he knelt beside Caden. The boy lay splayed open, eyelids droopy, lips parted on quick pants. His cock bobbed above his abdomen, eager to be toyed with. Tate wedged himself between Caden's legs and pushed on the back of one thigh to expose Caden's hole more. He worked one slick finger past the puckered ring.

As usual, the slave accepted the intrusion with little resistance. Tate added a second finger to stretch the entrance, which had the added benefit of allowing him to work the boy's prostate with his long middle finger. Caden moaned and arched his back. The slave was so sensitive to Tate's touch. It wouldn't take much of this type of attention to make him come. That was a temptation the was hard to resist. Still, he did, because he wanted to feel the boy's climax while buried inside him. And never a patient man to begin with, it had been too long for him to wait. As Tate pulled his fingers back out, Caden clenched around them as if he could trap them where the guy wanted them to be.

Tate smacked one ass cheek with a chuckle. "Greedy boy. I'm about to give you something much better."

Caden's answer was a low moan.

The brief prep wasn't going to be enough to help Caden take Tate's dick. It was long and thick. He knew his lovers had trouble adjusting to it. He sensed, however, that Caden wouldn't mind the difficulty.

"Do you like it rough? The burn of being stretched, I mean." He held his breath as he waited for an answer, hoping it would be a truthful one.

"Yes. Please." The tone and the expression when the answer came left no doubt of his sincerity.

Tate didn't press the matter. He didn't think he could wait even if he thought he should. Using both hands, he bowed Caden's legs back. Then he used his hips to line his cock up against the hole and thrust it in without a moment's hesitation. He kept going, grunting against the vise-like grip of the slave's channel, and didn't stop until he was balls-deep. The exquisite pleasure of being enveloped in the wet heat he'd anticipated forced his eyes shut. He held that position, simply savoring what it was like to be fucking someone again. It made him feel alive, like he had when he'd stood at the top of the run. This time, however, he knew the adventure could lead only to success.

Caden's breath caught against the pain of the sudden invasion. His hole was being stretched to an almost unbearable degree and his ass felt as if it were being split in two. He *loved* it. Being impaled by a man's cock while held in place by his hard grip was what he'd always craved. This, this control, this conquering by another was why he'd always chased older men. It was dominance more than age, he realized, that he needed. Young as he was, Tate was masterful, strong even in his weakened state. Caden didn't think he could break free even if he tried. Which he didn't. Instead, he submitted, taking deep breaths and relaxing his hole.

Tate barked out a breath. "God, you're tight. I want to fuck you hard and fast."

"Do it." Caden reversed his earlier efforts and instead clenched around the thick cock to feel it as much as he had initially. He drew his knees closer to his head to provide even better access to give Tate a bit more space to drive his cock. "Make me feel every inch of you."

Tate opened his eyes and stared down at him with an intensity that sent a chill up Caden's spine. Then he pulled back slowly until just the head of his dick remained inside…and held that position until Caden wanted to weep in frustration, before slamming into him again.

That was all the teasing his master was going to give him, give either of them. From that point on, Tate pounded into him with fast, deep thrust, snapping his hips to pound against Caden's ass. His eyes slammed shut as he grunted at the assault. It allowed him to feel, just feel, to narrow his concentration to that one spot where their bodies joined. Nothing else existed at that moment, nothing else mattered. All his fears and anger got shoved aside by the relentless wave of pleasure building within him. The repeated scraping of his prostate as Tate drove his dick in and out made his balls cramp. His cock ached and pulsed above his stomach. He couldn't reach it to jerk himself even if he'd wanted to. His hands were too busy holding him into a tight ball to give Tate a clear and easy shot at his hole. He gritted his teeth against the mounting pressure. Then an orgasm burst out of him without warning or any touching required. Caden tossed his head back as he howled out his climax.

And still, Tate kept on going, drilling Caden into the mattress as promised, even as he tossed his head and felt his muscles weakening. He couldn't hold on anymore. Just as his fingers lost their grip, the cock invading his channel swelled and pulsed. Cum splashed inside him. Tate shouted loud enough that the whole island probably could hear. It didn't matter. This was what Caden had been sent here to do. He was Tate's toy, and as the spasms of the man's dick subsided, he reveled for the first time in his fate. This was what he wanted, to be used and please a man, and be given pleasure in return. When Tate collapsed on top of him, he wrapped his arms around his master's sweaty back and hugged him close.

They lay like that for a long while, catching their breath, limbs entangled. That was how he realized Tate's shoulder was twitching and his leg trembled. Concerned, Caden managed to roll Tate onto his back.

"We overdid it. You're not healed well enough for that kind of strenuous sex. We've risked setting you back."

Part of him felt guilty. The other dared to think that the longer Tate needed to recover, the more time he had with the man, and could even pretend that he would spend his ten years right here with him. A stupid thing to allow into his brain. That was not going to happen, if for no other reason than Tate himself didn't want to stay any longer than he had to. There was a whole world out there that served as the man's playground. He could have any man he wanted to. Rich ones, like him. Educated ones. Free men, not slaves. He was a fool if he thought Tate's friendliness now meant anything more than making a bad situation more tolerable.

Tate grinned with his eyes still closed. "I love taking risks. You know that."

"Well, I don't." Annoyed at his fanciful musing as much as Tate's cavalier attitude, he hopped off the bed and went to get cleaned up.

He took care of himself first, wiping away the cum on his torso and around his hole. It was tender from the rough fuck, but he didn't care. He liked how he'd be feeling this for hours, if not days. And having a man's cum seeping from his ass reminded him of the good days, when sex was new and fresh and full of promises. He refused to dwell on how that craving for physical attention had led him to this terrible position in life. For now, he was living in paradise with Tate, someone who'd proved more appealing and kinder than he could have hoped for. There was no use fretting over the fact that his time with the guy was short-lived, that he didn't belong to him, and that his fate remained up in the air.

Focusing on the buzz of great sex, he filled a bowl with warm water and soaped up a washcloth. Tate had his eyes closed and was so boneless that he appeared to be sleeping. Caden approached the bed softly, intending to do only a quick wash up so as not to disturb him more than necessary.

"I'm awake." Tate opened one eye. "You don't have to sponge me down like I'm still an invalid."

"I like doing it." That was the truth and it surprised him as much as it must have Tate. A few weeks of getting to know each other had brought out the best in both of them.

He sat on the edge of the bed and placed the bowl on the nightstand. Tate's spent cock lay against his thigh, still shiny from its recent activity. Caden carefully wiped it clean then, rinsing out the cloth, removed the remnants of soap. The dick twitched at the simple touch, trying to rally. He couldn't help smiling because not only did it mean Tate wanted him again, but it also showed that he was recovering well.

Tate grabbed his wrist when Caden started to rise.

"Just toss that in the bowl and lie down next to me."

"As much as I appreciate the interest, you've had enough exertion for the day."

Tate sighed noisily. "Don't I know it. I'm not trying for round two. I only want you to sleep here…with me. In this bed."

Caden eyed the cot that had been brought in the second day so that he could be near to his master without having to sleep on the floor. As those things went, it was pretty comfortable. Tate's bed was better, of course, if for no other reason that they would be sharing it. Snuggling with another man was something he enjoyed and it had been forever. The appropriateness of sharing a bed was dubious, however. It seemed…too intimate, and with everyone on the island working for Tate's parents, he was sure the information would get back to them. And then what? He was supposed to be the equivalent of a living blow-up doll, not a true lover to him. Although there was no overt prohibition on his sleeping with the man, he somehow worried that it wouldn't be taken well. That it would be seen not as a convenience for his master, but a sign their relationship had become too personal.

The Grahams would not like that at all. Those fuckers counted on Tate having no allies here.

"I should sleep on the cot. You don't need me jarring you all night."

Tate tightened his grip. "I want you here. I get to decide, don't I?"

Caden dropped his gaze. "We both know that's not entirely true."

"My parents can go fuck themselves. They gave you to me, so I get to do whatever I want with you." He loosened his grip and ran his thumb over Caden's inner wrist. "Whatever *we* decide we want to do. Come on." He tugged hard enough to force him to lie down.

Not that it took much effort or convincing. Caden wanted to lie here, next to Tate's hard body. He turned on his side to face him. "Okay, whatever you say. I just don't want to make waves, I guess."

Tate drew him in closer and hugged him as if nothing hurt, which Caden knew couldn't be the case.

"I'm going to take care of you. I know we've danced around this topic a bit, but I've made up my mind. I'm not going to let my parents sell you off once I'm ready to leave."

Caden lightly clasped the man's hip. "How will you stop them? They'll extract a high price to agree." He could only imagine their using him to force Tate to come to heel, and he didn't want that. Maybe it was foolish to worry about this entitled man when his own future was so precarious. And yet, he couldn't help it.

"You let me worry about that. Jimmy was great at manipulating them, always getting his way while convincing them that he was only being a dutiful son. I learned a thing or two watching him. I've just been too angry to be clever, choosing instead to fight them overtly. With the right incentive, I can switch tactics."

"Am I that?" he dared to ask.

"Yeah." Tate kissed him, lightly. "You've grown on me," he added with a wry smile. "We can have fun together. I'll take you all over the world."

"I'd like that, so long as you don't expect me to do all those dangerous things with you. I'm more of a sit curled up in a chair sort of guy."

"I noticed, babe. Don't worry, you can greet me at the finish line or by the fire or in bed, whatever makes sense for what I'm doing. You can kiss my bruises and make me feel better." He shot him a leering grin.

"Okay. But please don't get hurt like this again. Wiping your ass is not my favorite thing."

Although he made light of it, he really didn't like the idea of watching Tate risk his life in all the ways he did merely for the thrill of it, to remind him he was still alive and as a big middle finger to his parents. And it wasn't only because he didn't want to be at the mercy of the Grahams again. It was more than that. He genuinely didn't want to see Tate hurt. There was no point in saying any of that, naturally. Even Tate wasn't going to appreciate his slave trying to dictate to him.

Tate yawned loudly before saying, "Funny, because I apparently love pounding yours."

With that, he dropped like a stone into sleep.

Caden closed his eyes to do the same, trying not to worry about the future. He had a feeling it wasn't going to be as easy as Tate imagined, either, to manipulate his parents. But it was all beyond his control, so there was no point in dwelling on what might be. Living in the moment was all he could do.

* * * *

Two knocks sounded from the other side of the inner door. "Breakfast, Mr. Tate."

Tate slammed into Caden with one final forceful thrust that left him unable to breathe. The man uttered a low growl, audible to Caden only, as he emptied himself. Caden had nothing left to release, given that with his cock trapped between his body and the mattress, it had been rubbed into two orgasms already.

"Leave it," Tate hollered out. "We'll serve ourselves."

The servant uttered a short acknowledgment of the order, then there was silence from the sitting room. Good thing they'd taken to eating in there now that

Tate was able to get out of bed. The closed door notwithstanding, the bedroom must reek of sex, given how the recovering Tate had woken with sufficient vigor to flip a still-sleeping Caden onto his stomach and impale him with his dick. As wake-up calls went, there was nothing to complain about. His life as a slave had taken a decided turn for the better.

With a groan, Tate eased out of him and rolled onto his back. "I hadn't realized how good morning sex could be. I don't usually spend the night with my lovers." He eyed Caden. "Was that all right? I didn't exactly get consent before spearing you."

Caden pushed up on his elbows with a chuckle. "The poor maid is going to have to deal with some very sticky sheets. Does that answer your question? Besides," he couldn't help adding. "I'm a slave. You don't need to ask permission to use me, remember?"

Tate winced. "I was an asshole when you first arrived. Please don't think that was the real me, and this is just me having a niceness interlude before going back to being a shithead again. Regardless of what the law says, I don't have a right to treat you like an object. If I get out of line, call me out on it. Okay?"

Caden grinned. "Okay." He considered the wisdom of exposing himself to someone with such power over him, then decided to be honest. "I kind of like being bossed around. It turns me on. In that sense, I guess becoming a slave makes more sense than my being born privileged."

"Hey!" With a frown, Tate ran a finger down his cheek. "Fantasies that get your rocks off are way different than being legally required to obey." He sat up. "I know. How about we give you a safeword? That way, if I'm doing something you don't like, we have a fool-proof method for your telling me to knock it off."

Caden pushed himself onto his knees. "I've never had one before. I'm not really into BDSM, just a bit of rough fucking."

"That's good to know. I'm not into that either, really, even though fucking a guy fast and hard is also what I enjoy. This situation isn't too different than the world of BDSM, though. You're literally legally obligated to obey me no matter what. You've not supposed to refuse even if you really don't like something, so how do I know if you don't? Seems like a safeword applies to this situation."

"That's a fair point." He shrugged. "Pineapple, I guess. I don't really like the taste of it, so…"

Tate pulled him in for a quick kiss. "Perfect. Let's shower, then eat. I know Ernesto is coming after lunch to torture me with new exercises. How about a walk after breakfast? I can show you the island."

Caden followed him into the bathroom. "I'd like that, so long as you don't overdo it."

"You can *pineapple* me if I do. Seems like a safeword is a smart thing to have all around." Tate went over to the huge walk-in shower and started the water flowing.

Caden leaned against the bathroom wall, preparing to enjoy the view of his master washing up. "I don't think that's how safewords are supposed to work."

"Why not? It's a way to emphasize to someone that they have to stop. Works for me," he added with a shrug. "Come on in."

"You want to shower together even though we just fucked?"

"Sure. I like being with you even when we're not having sex and this thing's big enough to fit a family of five. It'll be fun." He raised his eyebrows. "Have you ever gotten it on in one before?"

Caden pushed off the wall and padded over. "Yes, but I usually end out on my knees, sucking my partner off, or you know, jerking off the way we did before."

Tate shot him a wicked grin. "Any and all ways work for me."

Caden rolled his eyes. "Jesus. I think it was better for me when you needed your ass wiped."

"I don't hear a pineapple in that observation." Tate held out his hand.

Caden took it. "No. You don't." He laughed as he got pulled into the steam.

Chapter Seven

Tate had forgotten how beautiful the island was. He hadn't been there voluntarily in a long while. Too tame for his needs. There was nothing to offer the thrills he craved, and this recent trip had been forced on him, so his mood had been too sour to appreciate anything. With Caden by his side, however, he could afford to let go of the anger and find new admiration for the paradise that his prison was. And given the crushed shell and paved stone paths that had been laid all over the place, the walk wasn't too taxing. The only thing marring the morning was catching sight of the armed guards stationed around the house and the ports of entry. Even knowing that this wasn't a new security measure to keep him in, it still bothered him. He didn't have to be told to know that these men were under orders to make sure he didn't leave as much as they were to make sure no unauthorized people came in.

He stopped at the railing at the back of the house and pointed to the dock below. "That's where the fishing boats are kept. It's one of the few staples that are provided by the island staff, instead of being motored over from St. Thomas."

There was a set of stairs leading down but he didn't think he was quite up to making the trip. His weakness bothered him. *Got to be patient.* Not his strength, patience. He'd liked to keep moving, even before the accident that had left him an only child and under the scrutiny of parents who he knew resented his survival. Inactivity annoyed him, and without being at his best, he was at the mercy of others. That situation was intolerable. Except he wasn't alone anymore.

Caden stood next to him, close enough for the boy's heat to mix with the sultry air of the island and seep into Tate's battered body. It was comforting. Too much so, if he let himself dwell on it. He wasn't used to having someone there for him. Not even Jimmy had provided that much companionship. This slave did, however. *No, not slave.* He hadn't given much thought to the newish slave laws. On principle, the idea repelled him. His privileged life was a stroke of luck. But for that, he might have ended up in a desperate situation like Caden, forced to choose between what? Destitution, homelessness, or enslavement? There had to be a better way to help people than leaving them with those eventualities.

He didn't want to be part of that system and accept Caden as a slave. What was he then? Friend? Not really. They didn't know each other well enough or at all under conditions where they were both free to associate with each other or not. Lover? Sort of. The sex had gone from a holistic approach to relieving pain and boredom to off-the-charts pleasure. Caden seemed to really enjoy it, too. He'd dropped to his knees in the shower and sucked another orgasm out of Tate's tired body with an enthusiasm that had made him literally dizzy. And had then volunteered to wash him from head to toe with an attentive gentleness that had reminded Tate of his childhood nanny's efforts.

But so long as Caden was officially a slave, nothing he did could be taken at face value. Maybe there was no need to label what they had at the moment anyway. Caden was simply that—Caden. Seeing the island with his fresh eyes made Tate happy. That was something he hadn't felt outside a thrilling activity since before Jimmy's death. It was…nice. Caden had seeped past part of the hard shell Tate had erected around himself in the last ten years.

The boy in question put his chin on his palm as he leaned against the railing. "I've never seen anything so beautiful that it kind of makes my eyes hurt to look at. I mean, that water! It takes my breath away."

Yeah, Tate knew exactly what he was talking about, and that small observation caused his emotional barriers to buckle a bit more.

"I know just what you mean. Jimmy and I used to sail around this island all day when we came here as a family. Our parents were either sunning themselves by the pool or inside working. I don't know why they bothered to buy this place. They could have done that at our main residence in Boston just as easily."

Caden placed his hand on top of his. "Would you like to go out on the water? I understand how you don't want to but I'm a pretty good sailor myself. And there'd be no question about your being in command. We'd only go as far as you decide and come in whenever you say so."

Tate didn't realize he was turning his hand to entwine their fingers until it happened. He had to push the words past the lump in his throat that came from the incredibly sweet offer by this person who owed him nothing. He also couldn't suppress the sudden fear churning in his gut. It overrode any other feeling he had. This was the one thing he couldn't do anymore. Not since Jimmy's death had he set foot in anything with a sail. He didn't much care for motored vessels, either, but his parents' yacht was tolerable. It was ridiculous, really. Being out in a large sailboat in the ocean wasn't even nearly as risky as the other sports he tackled. And in this, he'd have Caden to support him. That was no small thing at this point. Yet, he still couldn't work up the nerve to do it. Probably never would.

"Thanks, but I'm going to have to pineapple that idea. I'm not… It would be too much of a strain—physically, I mean." It was pride that made him lie. Stupid, really, to be embarrassed to admit the truth to someone who already knew about his fear. He'd told no one other than Caden, though. And while his parents hadn't said as much, he figured they were just as happy that he didn't do the one thing that had killed their other son. In any event, no one brought the topic up. Not that they had ever been the kind of family to have heartfelt conversations. This near-phobia of sailing was a secret weakness that he'd kept to himself to the benefit of everyone. What if he took the chance and panicked while out in the boat? Caden would probably be able to bring them back to the dock, but others might notice his reaction and report it back to his parents.

Caden squeezed his hand. "You can just say no to my suggestions. I don't think this is a pineapple situation."

Tate gave a last look at the boats bobbing the water. "You're the only person besides me that could appreciate how much it is exactly that." He turned to walk back to the house before Caden could offer up the comfort Tate could see coming. "How about a swim in the pool before lunch and the next torture session."

Caden laughed. "That sounds good. Outside of a few vacations, I haven't had much chance to enjoy a pool outside."

"Really? From what you've said, I had the impression your family was rich enough to have one."

"That's mostly true. I mean, we weren't Graham-level rich, but very well off." Caden shrugged. "I can't remember the house we lived in while my mother was alive. It may have had a pool, but after her death, I spent the school year boarding at a place with only an indoor pool and summers at camp, swimming in a lake. I've been to beaches, of course, with salt water. I prefer freshwater swimming."

"Where was your father living all that time? Didn't you spend any holidays or vacations with him?"

Caden didn't answer right away. A sad look crossed his face before he chased it away with a grin. "Nope. When he wasn't working, he was lying between some really age-inappropriate model's legs. Dad liked them young, beautiful and dumb. Not that I had any chance to meet them, not even the one he actually married. I mean, I saw her at his funeral. We didn't have much to talk about, not surprisingly. What I know about his life I learned mostly from gossip sites, because my classmates made sure that I saw them. Everyone was both amused and in awe of my father's conquests."

"Really? That must have sucked, having your family life out on the internet. My parents pay a ton of money every year to keep their names out of the spotlight. Maybe that's why I never had any interest in surfing those kinds of websites or reading the gossip rags. I have no interest in keeping up with the Kardashians, let alone anyone else. That includes myself. I never read the stories I know are out there about my exploits. It really pisses my parents off how much press I get now." While he didn't say it out loud, he wondered what was worse—a parent who ignored you or ones that hovered and tried to control your every move?

Caden tossed his head. "It was fine, really. I remember being sad when my mother died, but when the old man did, I felt nothing. Well, maybe happy, actually, because he did leave me most of his estate, and not much to the woman he'd ended up marrying. I guess he wasn't totally enthralled to his dick."

"Money does equal freedom."

"And debt leads to enslavement." There wasn't as much bitterness in that statement as Tate might have expected.

"Did that asshole you hooked up with really leave you with nothing?"

Caden barked out a laugh. "Oh, how I wish he had merely wiped me out. No. He managed to take out credit cards and mortgage my townhouse without my even knowing it because I'm a moron who allowed him access to my computer. And he kept me dazzled, pacified and isolated with sex. I woke up one morning alone and with creditors banging on my door. Even selling every asset I possessed didn't cover the extent of the debt and, as he'd put it all in my name, I was on the hook. No one was sympathetic to how I'd been swindled by my fuck buddy. In fact, they thought I'd been in on it, deliberately screwing over everyone."

Tate stopped and pulled Caden in for a hug. "That is horrible. I'm so sorry."

He wanted to say more, do more, now that he had the boy in his arms. A flash of movement caught his eye and, dropping his hands, he stepped away from Caden as a guard rounded a bend in the walkway.

The man nodded. "Mr. Tate."

He glared back, unable to be civil to someone he knew wouldn't hesitate to strong-arm him if necessary. When he was sure they were alone again, he clasped Caden's hand and continued walking toward the house.

"Am I supposed to feel safer with those guys walking around with automatic weapons?"

"Under normal circumstances, yes. There are pirates in the Caribbean and they don't always confine themselves to the water."

"I know. I saw all the movies." Caden laughed as he hip-checked him.

Tate returned the bump. "Ha, ha." He sobered up. "For the moment, I'm imprisoned here. I'm sure they have orders to keep me from taking the launch or the sea plane."

"Can you pilot a plane?"

"Sure. I started parachuting as the first real thrill activity after…after Jimmy died, and I decided that I wanted to be able to fly my own plane, too."

"Compared to the other stuff you do, both of those things sound tame." Caden hesitated before adding,

"Do you really believe that if you tried to leave, these guards would stop you with force?"

Tate grimaced. "Without a doubt."

"But that's like…illegal, isn't it? Kidnapping, false imprisonment. Are all these people willing to risk breaking the law for the sake of your parents?"

"We Grahams have always known that paying well for loyalty is the smart move. And once they have their claws in someone, hanging the loss of their job over them helps convince even the most reluctant ones."

"Even Miss Ophelia?"

"Even her," he confirmed with a nod. "She has two kids in college right now, learning how to pave a more prosperous path. Plus aging parents of her own that she has to take care of. She can't afford to jeopardize any of her obligations."

Caden was silent for a while, no doubt digesting that uncomfortable truth.

"Can't you simply offer to pay them more? Like how they do in spy movies?"

"I could. But my folks have *billions*. My grandmother left me about seventy-five million, which is a fortune, but it can't compete with their resources. Plus, they've spent years cultivating connections with powerful people. One word whispered in the right ear can make or break someone's entire future."

"It's not right."

Tate shook his head. "No, it isn't." His current predicament and its effects on everyone else on the island couldn't be helped at the moment. He needed to fully recover before he would have the power to change this situation. Railing against it wasn't going to help anyone.

"They can't keep me here forever, thank God. Once I'm fully recovered, they'll send for me and try to convince me to give up my pastimes. I bet they think my extended recovery in isolation will cause me to dwell on the error of my ways. They don't know me very well," he said in his best Bugs Bunny voice.

Caden chuckled. "No, they don't. Except, what if they do? What if they try to keep you here for the rest of their lives?" There was a real look of concern on his face.

"That won't happen. They need my face to turn up at meetings and social events. Otherwise, difficult questions will arise. And I do indulge them from time-to-time at those activities. I mean, I get that I have to run our businesses at some point. So…once I'm back in civilization, I can regain control over my life. I just have to be patient. Good thing I have great company." He tugged Caden to pick up the speed. "Come on. This walk has made me hungry. If we eat lunch early, we'll have time to fuck before Ernesto arrives."

Caden laughed. "I feel like I created the proverbial monster."

Tate laughed too, except he knew that it had been his parents who had warped him into someone he didn't like very much. For the first time in years, he was beginning to believe he could be something else. Something better.

* * * *

Caden watched Tate as he sliced into the water from the diving board with Olympic-level grace. The guy performed everything he did with tremendous skill and talent. His dreaded check-in calls with Tate's parents gave him access to Miss Ophelia's tablet and she didn't always come to fetch him right away. It had allowed him time to surf so he'd given into the temptation to do some internet sleuthing on his master in the early days. He couldn't resist learning as much as he could about the man he catered to. There was so much about Tate to be found that he hadn't been able to scratch the surface. The paparazzi loved him. Not only did Tate participate in risky sports, he often did them well enough to win. There were countless pictures of him hoisting some kind of trophy or another. And his movie-star looks made him a sought-after celebrity in his own way. Groupies of both genders flocked to his events, even though he was open about being gay. He simply had a universal appeal and people loved to orbit him.

His parents might pay to keep their lives private, but Tate kept the Graham name in the spotlight. *They must hate it.* Not only was their surviving child ignoring the family businesses, he was also dragging their name in public in ways they probably thought of as vulgar. Maybe if he'd stuck with one sport and had won an Olympic medal or two, it might be different. But Tate flitted from one sport to the other, as if flaunting his wealth and ignoring any responsibilities to his family or anyone else. Caden had found only cursory stories about Tate acting like the scion of two vast business empires.

Funny how buying human beings to serve them was acceptable and proper, even when acquiring a whore, while racing around in the mud on a motorbike was déclassé. The Grahams had a warped sense of morality, or really no morality at all. Money and status were what mattered. At first, Tate had seemed to be the same. Not anymore. Caden was sure now that the man was a decent person and didn't deserve his confinement. Caden was worried about him, which was crazy, because he was in far more danger than Tate was.

Stewing over the possible future was pointless as there was nothing he could do to help either of them, as he was constantly reminding himself these days. With the setting sun still sparkling on the water and the scent of dinner on the air, he only needed to live in the moment and enjoy what he could. He treaded water by the side of the pool, watching Tate swim like a fish toward him. The guy popped up and immediately grabbed him by the waist. Caden had only a second to take a big gulp of air before he was dragged under. Tate held him close, entwining their bodies, and spun them in a slow circle under water. They both kept their eyes open and as they stared and grinned, cocooned in their own world, something inside Caden tripped like a switch. He didn't merely *like* Tate now, a deeper feeling took hold. A brief vision of their staying on the island forever popped into his head. Even recognizing how foolish the idea was, he clung to it as much as he did Tate's body.

The need to breathe forced them to the surface. Tate didn't let go of him, however, and Caden wasn't inclined to break apart, either. Instead, they treaded water in each other's arms. Tate pulled him even closer for a kiss. The open display of affection made Caden a little fearful, but he was hopeless to resist the man. And he felt safe with him in many ways. Despite his recent injuries, Tate remained incredibly jacked, his arms easily holding Caden above the surface. He also followed his master's lead when it came to judging what was acceptable to do and where.

They both became aroused quickly, their hard dicks bumping through their swimming trunks. Tate tightened his leg around Caden's to grind their lower halves. The friction was a delightful tantalization. He had visions of their swimming over to the pool's edge, of Tate turning him around to expose his ass and plunging into it. The mere thought had him groaning long and low.

"Well, well, nice to see you up and about and taking advantage of your toy."

They propelled apart at the sound of Harding's voice, Tate swiping his hair off his face to glare up at the man standing by the side of the pool. Caden kept his gaze down and kicked over to the farthest edge. His heart scrambled like a terrified hamster trapped in a small cage, even as he trusted Tate to take care of any trouble coming their way.

"Harding. What are you doing here?" Contempt dripped from Tate's tone.

"Checking up on how you are doing. Much improved, I can see." The man's eyes were hidden by sunglasses but his smirk said it all.

"I'm sure Miss Ophelia, the nurse and Ernesto have been providing detailed reports. No need for you to risk your Brioni suit wilting in this climate."

The asshole did look ridiculous dressed as he was in clothing one would expect to find in a plush high-rise office. His presence here couldn't be a good development. Caden hated him, and hadn't forgotten how he'd used him as living porn on the plane. Although the glasses kept the man's eyes hidden, Caden couldn't help feeling as if he were being scrutinized with scorn. He bit his lip to keep silent. Nothing he could say or do would be helpful. He had to leave it up to Tate to deal with the prick.

"Your parents wanted a more…*dispassionate* assessment. Your caregivers have either clouded judgment or a vested interest in your remaining under their care."

Tate bared his teeth. "Yeah? I guess it didn't occur to them to pick up the phone and ask me directly. Or, here's a thought—they could come and see me themselves. Too busy, I guess. And why should they bother when they have a lapdog like you to do tiresome things for them. You can tell them that not only am I recovered enough to leave, I insist upon it."

Harding smiled, like a shark, letting the insult slide off him like water. "Good to hear…*sir*. I'll convey the message and oh, and if you're ready to go home, you won't be needing the slut. I'll take him with me. Plenty of people to fuck back in Boston, after all. You don't need to settle for this piece of trash."

Caden couldn't hold back a gasp and now his heart felt frozen with fear.

Tate let out what sounded like a growl. "Fuck off, Harding. He stays with me."

The Grahams' enforcer paced lazily down the length of the pool, then back again, his sightless gaze seeming to swing between Tate and Caden. "Why? Your parents bought a slave to keep you occupied while you were an invalid. If you're not that anymore, you don't need him. I'm sure his resale value remains high, and I know Gordon Baker is always looking for a new diversion."

Tate streaked across the pool with startling speed. He proved how recovered he was by hoisting himself out of the water. "Get the fuck out of my sight,

Harding." He only had to take one step toward the man to make him back-up. "I hope my parents are paying you well because once I'm in charge, the first thing I'll do is kick your bony ass to the curb."

Harding held out his hand. "Calm down, for Christ's sake. You've obviously formed an attachment to the boy. I'll let the bosses know…about everything."

What the man said and the way he said it caused Caden's stomach to drop. His time in paradise and with Tate was coming to an end. He was sure of it.

Tate took another step with his hands clenched. Harding didn't wait to hear or say more. Turning, he fled as fast as someone could go while still keeping some semblance of dignity.

Tate went over to the edge where Caden remained afloat and held out his hand. "Come on, let's shower and dress for dinner."

Caden accepted the help and marveled at how easily Tate essentially pulled him out.

"Don't worry about that fucker." Tate carded Caden's hair away from his face. "We'll be getting out of here soon. My place in Boston isn't as fabulous as this but we'll have a lot more to do while I finish my recovery." He stated all of this as fact.

Oh, how Caden wanted to believe him. "I don't think your parents are going to let me stay with you."

"Don't worry about them. They want to rein me in and that gives me leverage to get what I want, too."

Now Caden was alarmed. "You're not going to give into them for me, are you?" The idea both appalled and cheered him. "I mean, you want to live your life your way. Don't let them use me as a carrot. Or a stick."

Tate surprised him by lowering his head and sweetly kissing Caden. "I like you. More than." He sighed. "Being with you, these last several weeks have been the happiest of my life since losing Jimmy. And maybe…maybe I'm not as sanguine about risking my skin as I once was. Leading a more sedate life might not be so bad if I have someone to enjoy it with."

Caden couldn't hold the smile back. No matter what happened, hearing that Tate liked him was enough for him to let go of the fear. "Do you think we have time for another shower-based blow job before dinner?"

By way of an answer, Tate let out a whoop and hurried Caden back to their room.

Chapter Eight

Tate forced his eyes open, his mouth dry and his head aching. He was hungover in a major way even though he couldn't remember drinking much. *Or at all.* He pushed up on his elbows and glanced at the other side of the bed, expecting to see Caden sprawled on his stomach as usual. Except there was no one there. He sat bolt upright and looked around the room, his head swimming a bit at the sudden movement.

"Caden?"

No answer came. Throwing the sheet aside, he got out of bed, noticing for the first time that he had on sleep pants. He frowned. That was odd. Since Caden had started sleeping with him, in the figurative and literal sense, he'd gone to bed naked. They both did. He loved being able to reach out and touch the boy's silky skin and sink them both deep into pleasure without any encumbrances.

Confused and a little alarmed, he stumbled into the bathroom. It was empty. He took only a few seconds to relieve himself before he raced to the sitting room. Caden was not there, either, and now panic started to push through. Not since he'd arrived had the slave gone anywhere without him. No, that wasn't true. He'd left the suite to video chat with his parents a few times, spinning half-truths about what was going on with Tate. That was where he was. Miss Ophelia had him in her quarters to make the report. They hadn't woken him because there was no need to. Better to let him sleep off his hangover…except he hadn't been drinking, damn it. He was sure of it.

Maybe he'd relapsed without knowing it, his injuries kicking him in the balls one last time, forcing him to bed. He groped at his collarbone and leg. Other than a few twinges and the ropey scars of his skin still healing, everything felt fine. Still, there was a simple explanation for Caden's absence. His parents wanted an update from the slave after getting Harding's report. That was all.

"Shit!" *Harding.* Tate's knees threatened to buckle. He managed to pound the call button before he lowered himself into a chair and took deep breaths to calm down.

It didn't surprise him when Miss Ophelia responded instead of a maid. Her expression confirmed the worst.

"Where is he?" For the first time in his life, he didn't speak to the woman in a respectful tone.

"I'm sorry, Mr. Tate. Harding took him away last night."

"Last night!" He jumped to his feet and didn't care when it startled the housekeeper. "How? What happened? Why do I feel hungover?"

"I'm so, so sorry."

"Stop saying that and tell me!"

Miss Ophelia closed her eyes briefly. "We had orders. The nurse spiked your after-dinner coffee so that you'd fall asleep. Harding and the guards took Caden. They didn't hurt him," she was quick to add. "He went with them without a fight. You don't have to worry about him."

Tate let out a string of curses, not caring that the proper older woman winced at them. "What?" he yelled. "You don't like bad words, but drugging me and kidnapping Caden is perfectly okay? Is that what you'll be thinking when you motor to church next Sunday to pray to a God you still think exists in this fucked-up world? Holy fuck, what is wrong with all of you?"

The woman had the decency to look ashamed. Not that it mattered in the least.

"Mr. Tate, you have every reason to be mad, and I'm not going to excuse what we all did. I wish it could have been different. Maybe if you meet your parents halfway, you can forge a peaceful path forward."

"You're advocating I negotiate with terrorists? Because that's what they are. You think if I bend the knee to them, life will be better? For whom? It sure as hell won't be for me, having to knuckle under for fear that they'll take Caden away from me again."

Now the woman's expression turned truly bleak. "They won't be doing that. Your...affection for the slave is unseemly. He was only supposed to provide you with a diversion. They're selling him on, I believe."

His stomach dropped and his blood froze. "To whom?"

"I'm not sure."

"Tell me!"

Miss Ophelia covered her eyes. "Mr. Baker, according to what Mr. Harding said."

"Of course. Someone just as depraved as they are."

Tate hadn't thought he could feel worse, be swamped with greater fear. The growing sense of panic threatened to overwhelm him. Participating in risky sports had taught him how to push down fear and face things with a clear head. Caden needed him, depended on him for rescue whether he knew it or not.

"Get out. Have all my meals brought in here. I don't want to see any of you. And I'm no longer the compliant patient. Guess my parents jumped the gun on getting rid of Caden, huh?"

"Your PT…"

"Not your concern. Tell Ernesto he's out of a job. If I could fire the rest of you, I would. Now, do as I say."

The woman hesitated a moment, then complied.

Tate returned to his room to plan his escape. He could do this. No matter the obstacles, he would get off the island and go after Caden. At least he knew where the guy would be. Baker was a creature of habit, as much as any others of his class. He had a home for every season and this time of year, that meant he would be at his ski lodge in Hudson Valley. Tate had been there a few times, hating the man but loving the slopes. It was a few hours' flight time out of St. Thomas. Getting there would be a piece of cake once he got off the island. And that was the problem. There was only one way to do that if he wanted to avoid the guards, which he did. There was no chance of his truly getting hurt if he fought with them, but he was outnumbered and it wouldn't help Caden if he ended up locked in his suite or tied to his bed. Or even drugged into a stupor.

He wouldn't have thought they'd stoop so low, but apparently his parents still held surprises for him.

No, he had to be smart about this. And brave. Yeah, and not in the way he'd pretended he was being with his extreme sports. Those had been indulgences. This was real and serious. Caden's very life depended on what he did over the next twenty-four hours. Not that Baker would kill him, but the man would make the boy's life miserable. He knew the fucker enough to predict that. It couldn't happen. He wouldn't allow it to. For the first time since Jimmy's death, he had to get the fuck over himself and do what needed to be done.

* * * *

Caden spat the mouthful of cum into Harding's coffee cup and glared at the man, daring him to inflict punishment for the insolence. Harding sneered at him as he stuffed his dick back into his pants, but otherwise didn't make a move. He was sufficiently smart to not put a mark on Caden, however much was tempted to. On the island, the guards had been careful to herd Caden onto the plane without roughing him up. No doubt they were all under orders not to damage the merchandise. Because fuck, the Grahams had sold his contract. That was the only explanation for what was happening. They'd torn him from Tate's limp side with no explanation. The fact that no one was freaking out about Tate's sudden unconsciousness told him he'd been drugged. Harding's appearance with the guards, and the smug look on his face, confirmed how the plan was to separate them with as little drama as possible.

He had to blink back tears at the knowledge he would never see Tate again, never have the chance to confess his true feelings. Because seeing Tate go down suddenly and without any obvious explanation had cemented Caden's commitment. Friendship had morphed into budding love. He could trace the transition back to their time in the pool the previous day. Now, with Tate forever out of his reach, the tender emotion wouldn't be contained. But it did have to be hidden. Sharing his feelings by any look or word wouldn't do either him or Tate any good. Not wanting to show weakness in front of Harding, he scooted back to stand. Harding shoved him onto the floor of the plane with a casual press of his shoe against Caden's chest.

"Stay where you are, slut. I may want another blow job before we land." The asshole pressed the call button for the steward, who had discreetly hidden in the back of the plane when the party had begun. Harding waved at the cup. "Get me a new coffee."

The steward shot Caden a sympathetic look before hurrying to obey. Caden leaned against the opposite-facing chair with his legs bent, staring out of the window. There was nothing to see other than the darkness of night, but it was better than looking at his kidnapper.

"Did you fancy yourself Cinderella or something?" There was baiting amusement in the man's tone.

Caden ignored the rhetorical question and instead tried to make his mind go blank. Thinking of Tate hurt too much, and imagining his new future terrified him in a way that becoming a slave hadn't before. Then, he hadn't expected anything except unhappiness. Now that he'd had the benefit of being with a loving master like Tate, he knew his future was going to be unbearably bleak.

Harding took the new cup of coffee and waved the steward away. "I expect you imagined Tate would be your savior, that you could lie around his bed like some pampered concubine for the next ten years." The man barked out a laugh. "As if you were ever going to be anything more than a temporary diversion." He put the cup on its saucer and placed it on the table. Then crossed his legs, a man at ease and smugly content. "The Grahams were never going to permit that. They were very unhappy to hear about how…cozy you two had become."

Caden glared at him. "I bet you were the kid who always snitched on his classmates."

Harding smiled. "Better. I was the hall monitor and got to issue infraction tickets. I've always had a keen sense of the path to success. Unlike you." He looked out of the window. "Stupid boy. If you had behaved yourself, the Grahams would have sold you on to someone old and confined to his home who was looking for companionship. Instead, you've pissed them off, so now you belong to one of the meanest fuckers I've ever met. You're not going to like being Baker's whore, I can promise you that." He grinned before picking up his coffee and started to play with his phone.

Trying not to give into despair, Caden closed his eyes and dropped his head back onto the seat of the chair behind him.

He woke with a start when the steward nudged him kindly. Harding was fastening his seatbelt and the tilt of the plane told Caden they were descending. Pushing up from the floor, he sat down and strapped himself in. Outside, the night sky was still black. He wasn't sure how long they'd been traveling, but he couldn't see any lights below to indicate they were landing in Boston. A few minutes later, the plane touched the ground, and when it came to a stop, Harding got up without so much as a glance in Caden's direction.

It was the steward once again who helped him. The man handed him a down jacket and the burst of cold air that entered the plane when the outer door opened made Caden happy to have it. Stairs led to a tarmac of what appeared to be a regional airport. With it not being dawn yet, the place was pretty empty. Only a few maintenance people milled about. Caden pulled the jacket closed as a biting wind whipped through him.

He'd assumed they were heading to a car, but Harding strode toward a hangar area, the back of his camel-haired coat flapping behind him. Unlike Caden, the asshole had gloves and a scarf. Tucking his hands into his pockets, Caden nestled his chin into his collar and hurried to keep up. A helicopter soon came into view. They boarded it in silence and within minutes of landing, they were once more in the air.

Because he'd gone home with classmates for vacation a time or two, Caden wasn't unfamiliar with this mode of private transportation. He would have been thrilled with the ride if not for the circumstances. In the hazy light of the first signs of dawn, he spied a mountainous terrain, snow still blanketing the ground. He'd been on the island for so long, he'd forgotten that it was only early spring in the eastern part of the United States. It was impossible to say exactly where they were, but the trip hadn't been that long, so it had to be New England or New York. Although being curious about his location was better than focusing on the rank fear of his future, he didn't try to ask Harding any questions about where they were and where they were headed. Not only wouldn't he give the fucker the satisfaction of voicing his concerns, he also didn't have headphones on to communicate with anyone in the copter. The loud, steady whirl of the vehicle made it otherwise difficult to be heard. So, he sat back, waiting to find out what his new home was going to be, dreading meeting the man who now owned him.

The helicopter banked toward the side of a mountain. A huge chalet came into view, fitting snugly against a cliff in the back and boasting a rolling lawn in the front. Caden caught glimpses of an outside pool still covered for the winter, tennis courts and stables. The copter swooped over to a flat patch of ground with a landing pad built in. The pilot touched down with obvious skill and killed the motor. Harding jumped out and Caden had no choice but to follow him. Even with the sun peeking out, it was damn cold. Caden huddled into his jacket as he trailed behind Harding.

A golf cart, driven by a distinguished-looking older Asian man, pulled up to them. He was bundled up against the cold to a degree that his face was mostly covered. "Mr. Harding. I see you made good time." The man didn't seem happy about his early morning, frosty drive. He flicked his gaze at Caden, his expression reading as if he stared at a bug. "This is him, I take it."

Harding shoved Caden forward. "Good morning, Mr. Chau. You'll find that he can be difficult."

Chau smirked. "Well, Mr. Baker rather likes that type. Get in." His tone was icier than the temperature. "Thank you, Mr. Harding."

Before Caden could blink, Harding was heading back to the helicopter and Chau was turning the golf cart toward the chalet.

"Do not speak to me or anyone else unless you're answering a question. Do you understand?"

Did I look like I wanted to talk to you, fucker? Caden did his best to hide his disgust and bit back a retort that was dying to leap out of his head and onto his tongue. "Yes, sir." He wasn't going to have any friends here, that was obvious. There was no point in actively courting enemies. Maybe Chau was the kind of guy who could be coopted with secret blow jobs.

"Good. Mr. Baker is not in residence but he'll be back tomorrow. We need to get you cleaned up for him." He made it sound like Caden was contaminated or something.

As there hadn't been a question in that remark, Caden clamped his lips shut and stared at the beauty around him even as he knew he was being taken to ugliness.

* * * *

Tate settled his backpack across his good shoulder as he crouched behind the broad plants lining the terrace. It was a surprisingly moonless night with a thick cloud cover, a boon that almost made him believe there was a benevolent God looking out for him after all. This side of the island compound wasn't patrolled as heavily as the rest of it. The waters were too shallow and the coast was populated by hidden reefs that made it too treacherous for deep water boats to navigate. All that was here was the small dock for the sailboats that the family used for pleasure when in residence. Not that anyone did avail themselves of the luxury. Not anymore. Not since the accident. Himself in particular. That was probably another reason why there were no guards patrolling this area. No one was worried about him taking off in this manner. Although he'd never voiced his fears, he must have given clear signs of them anyway.

It didn't stop the boats from being maintained, the same way that every part of all the family homes were kept ready by a legion of servants as if the Grahams were in residence. So there it was, a nice little nine-footer that could be handled by a single person. It rocked against the dock, as if simply waiting for him to use it as his only way off the island — if he had the balls to take it. He gripped the strap of his pack and willed himself to stare at the boat. He let the images and sounds of the accident flood his brain as he knew they would. The wind of the storm lashed his face and chilled him to the bone. His scream of terror, mixed with Jimmy's, as their boat got tossed up and over a mammoth wave filled his ears with such force, he winced. He began to pant as he frantically called to Jimmy, his head whipping this way and that trying to glimpse him among the choppy water. It took nothing for him to send his mind back to those moments, to relive the worst moment of his life.

It was much harder to escape it and find his way back into reality. He tightened his grip on the straps of his pack with enough force to cause his fingernails to scrape his palms. Closing his eyes, he struggled to get his breath under control, and concentrated on the weight of his pack. Inside were stacks of bills from the family safe that would buy his way to Caden's rescue. He'd hoped to find his wallet so that he'd have his license and credit cards. It had been disappointing to find it wasn't stashed on the island, but the wads of cash his family always kept on hand — just in case —

would grease his way. Once he had Caden back, he'd go to his own lawyer to do what was necessary to free Caden legally and start the process of breaking away from his parents. That was the plan. All he had to do was follow through. This first part would be tough, but Caden was worth it.

"Pull yourself together, dickhead. This isn't so hard. Think of what Caden's going through, what he has to endure."

Thoughts of the boy being at Baker's mercy made him sick. It had been hard to force down some food to keep his energy levels up. Between memories of the accident and visions of the horrors Caden faced, his stomach was threatening to toss everything back up. Swallowing hard, he once more verbally kicked his own ass. Then, Tate moved to the steps leading down to the dock, staying low in case anyone in the house was up and looking out of a window. He kept his ears open for any sound of a guard's heavy tread. With only the faint glow from the outside lights to guide him, he crept down. At the terrace halfway from the dock, his heart nearly stopped. There, sitting quietly with only the light from her tablet making her visible, was Miss Ophelia. Tate froze, but not before she turned her head to look at him.

The woman stared at him for a second or two, then put her fingers first over her eyes, then covered one ear and finally tapped her lips before going back to reading her tablet.

It took Tate another moment to breathe a silent sigh of relief. *See no evil, hear no evil, speak no evil.* He got the message. There was absolutely no reason for the house manager to be out here, in the dark, with no view to speak of, instead of snuggling down in her own bed.

She was here because she knew he'd leave the island the only possible way. With her presence, she could shoo away any guards that might occasionally patrol this side during the night. It meant that she was going out on a limb for him as much as she dared. He mentally thanked her before continuing down to the dock.

He waited and looked and listened at the edge of the foliage. With no one stirring, he moved onto the dock and quickly went into the shed housing the sailing gear. It was nearly pitch-black inside, but it didn't take long for his eyes to adjust in order to see what he needed. He knew anyway from long experience how the shed was organized. Walking over to the mainsails, he touched the wrapped canvas, appreciating the visceral feel of the natural fibers his family always used. No polyester for the Graham family. There was the expected echo of his fear, but also something warm. He and Jimmy had loved sailing around the island. And this was how he would rescue Caden. As he caressed the sail, he imagined it was the boy's skin. His dick tightened, but so too did his heart. Being with Caden was not merely fun and sex. It was more. Far more. He had to get over his fear and get off the island.

With a renewed sense of purpose and the kind of calm that stole over him right before a risky activity, he grabbed what he needed and went out to the boat. A quick scan revealed that he was still alone. He hauled his gear onto the boat, automatically steadying himself with practiced ease as he tossed his pack down and got to work. Rigging the sail came as naturally to him as anything he'd ever done in life. His hands knew what to do without his brain needing to weigh in. As he worked, he went through each step he planned for how to reach Caden. He'd had time during the day to figure it out, and wanted to make sure he kept every phase of his journey clearly in mind. Before he knew it, the boat was ready to go. The sail flapped in the steady breeze.

He untied the line and jumped in by the tiller. Pushing off from the dock, he settled down, tightening the sail and steering into the wind. There was a motor, but of course, he didn't dare use it. If his escape was discovered, the launch on the other side of the compound would catch up to him easily. He didn't fancy his chances outrunning or outfighting the guards, and knew that he wouldn't be given another chance to slip his chains. He had to tamp down his impatience and let the Caribbean ocean breeze take him away. It was strong enough to get him to St. Thomas by morning. He'd put in as close to the airport as he could. There he could rent a plane to fly himself to New York. His face was familiar enough that he didn't think he'd run into any trouble. And of course, cash always eased the way. He knew where Baker's Hudson Valley home was located. He also knew it would be guarded. There was only one way to gain access without detection, the same way there'd been only one way for him to leave the island. Fortunately, that was only going to take skill to maneuver. Skill that he possessed.

It would not be fraught like this leg of the journey, where his personal demons kept trying to force him to turn around. His gaze darted about, looking for signs of dangerous winds picking up, or of tall waves that would wash him overboard. There was nothing, of course. The weather and sea were both calm.

"This isn't like then. There is no storm. I know what to do."

He concentrated on the task of keeping the boat on the fastest tack possible. And he pictured Caden, maybe being abused already. This time was going to be different. He was going to succeed. He was going to rescue the someone he loved.

Chapter Nine

Caden lay on his bed, reading some book on the history of Hudson Valley and watching the spring snow that was sprinkling the ground. He was bored, and that was a good thing. Baker had been delayed, giving him a days' worth of reprieve. Chau's orders kept him from leaving to explore the house and everyone ignored him other than coming to bring him food. He appreciated the solitude. It would end as soon as the master returned. And not in a good way. As nice as having his own room was, all of his clothing had been removed, with only a cotton robe provided by a footman. The reason for allowing him to cover up that much was soon apparent. He'd been brought to a medical room deep in the bowels of the house where a slick and gruff doctor had subjected Caden to a thorough and humiliating medical exam. Apparently Chau's idea of clean meant inside and out. Blood had been drawn and his ass had been explored for any signs of disease with far more interest by the doctor than seemed warranted. Bent over as he was, Caden couldn't see the man's face, but he could feel his nasty fingers probing and fondling. By the way he was huffing behind him, it seemed obvious the guy was getting off on it, too.

Finally, he'd been allowed to put the robe back on and return to his room to shower. A new robe replaced the first one once he was done. The way everyone acted, it was as if he'd been living in squalor instead of a luxury villa with someone Baker knew personally. Like he might bring cooties or something into the pristine opulence of the Baker chalet. Worse, keeping himself clean required a daily enema, and the implication of why made him shiver. It was proof that Baker intended to fuck him, and while that wasn't a surprise, it slammed home more than anything else how his life had changed. For the worse.

In the early moments of his enslavement, he wouldn't have given it much thought, especially as Baker clearly met his preferred type of being an older man. Now, though, he had experienced the joy of having an emotional and physical bond with someone that he'd fallen in love with. It was stupid that he'd done so, but it was no less true. He thought of himself as belonging to Tate, too, even though he'd never been legally owned by the guy. Blow jobs allowed him to remain detached. Being invaded by another man's dick was going to feel as if he were being defiled, no longer worthy of Tate. And it would be a form of cheating, at least within his own heart.

The drone of a helicopter met his ears and caused his stomach to drop. He knew without anyone having to tell him that the master had arrived. Who else but a wealthy person would choose such an expensive and planet-killing mode of transportation rather than being driven from the airport? Putting the book down, he swung his legs over the side of the bed and waited to be summoned. Try as he might, he couldn't calm his jittery stomach. Maybe he'd throw up on the guy. Wouldn't that be fun? Although it might lead to his being sold on. He wouldn't like his next owner any better, but it would buy him time.

It took longer than he expected for his door to swing open. No knocking here. Not for the likes of him. Chau entered with his usual expression of distaste, as if it were Caden's idea to be sullying the master's castle. He gestured for Caden to follow him, not bothering to waste his breath. He led Caden down not to the master's bedroom, which was a relief, but to what turned out to be a home office. Baker sat on a couch with a cut glass of amber liquid in his hand, despite it being the early afternoon.

Well, it's five o'clock somewhere, haha.

The man beckoned for Caden to come closer and perused him like something he was about to purchase. Something that he'd actually purchased, no doubt. Caden took the opportunity to do the same to his master. He was around the age of Tate's parents, middle-aged heading toward just old, built like a bear, and carried the supreme confidence of anyone in his position would. His big, boxy face was prominent, given the brush cut of his salt and pepper hair. He was more muscular than fat, and clothed in a well-cut suit that enhanced his masculinity. In another life, Caden would have welcomed the sight of him.

Not now. Not ever, even if he were a nice man. Which he wasn't. There was no question about that.

Baker flicked his gaze to Chau. "His tests came back negative?"

Chau nodded. "Yes, sir. And the doctor gave him a thorough exam." There was a hint of smugness in his tone, as if he knew the doctor had taken liberties.

Baker didn't seem to notice. Or maybe he didn't care. "Good. I'm particular about where I stick my dick." This unnecessary comment was directed at Caden. "You can go." That was to Chau. When the man was gone, the master said, "Take that off."

Caden didn't hesitate to obey. He shrugged off the robe and laid it across a chair. Then he stood gazing over Baker's head as the man stared at him. This was nothing. He'd been down this road already, being scrutinized. He briefly wondered if it were possible that Baker would reject him. But no, there was no point in hoping for a better situation. For someone like him, there wasn't one. *Except Tate.* He shrugged off the thought and instead made his expression as neutral as he could. There was still some pride left in him and he didn't want the man to know how gut-wateringly scared he was.

Baker sipped his drink. "Turn around."

Once more, Caden did as told, grateful that there was a fire blazing. The chalet had big rooms with high ceilings. Not a cozy spot to spend the night after a day of skiing. His skin pimpled from the cold.

Baker grunted. "Nice. I'm looking forward to pounding into that ass tonight. I'm going to beat it often, too. Just for fun—my fun—so don't think it's a punishment you can wheedle your way out of. You'll know when you've made me mad, but I bet you'll like the beatings when they're delivered because I'm happy."

Caden shivered at the man's words more than the cold. He was certain he wouldn't like being hit as a form of sex play, but there was no point in saying so.

"Come here."

Caden steeled himself as he turned around. He knew what was coming. Baker sat with his legs wide open, his designer slacks bulging from his erection.

The man patted his crotch and grinned. "You know what to do."

Yes, he did. With leaden feet, Caden went over and sank to his knees in the space between his master's legs. He tried to blank out all thoughts as he unbuckled Baker's belt, lowered the zipper and freed his cock. It was big. Really big, both long and thick. He bet the man was proud of what nature had given him, probably was the kind of guy who stood around naked in a locker room just to show his equipment off. Under other circumstances, Caden would have looked forward to the idea of being speared by such a dick. Now, it simply terrified him.

He refused to show his fear, however. Moistening his lips, he leaned over Baker's lap to clasp the shaft and lick the tip. This skin was clean, other than a bit of pre-cum. He appreciated that the taste of the blow job wasn't going to be nasty. Not that he would have expected it to be. Still, anything that made this experience less abhorrent was a blessing. Of course, there was nowhere to spit out the cum afterward, and even if there were, unlike Harding, Baker had nothing holding him back from delivering a hard rebuke. The man's big hands would hurt wherever his blow might land. Caden wouldn't benefit from trying to piss him off.

Baker grunted and bucked his hips in a silent command. Taking a deep breath, Caden opened his mouth as wide as possible to take as much of the dick as he could. The girth of the shaft stretched his lips painfully wide. The heavy cock weighed his tongue down. He sucked hard and jerked the dick with his hand to make quick work of the job. When the bulbous head hit the back of his throat, he gagged and pulled away to breathe more easily.

Except Baker wasn't having any of that delicacy. He fisted Caden's hair with his free hand, the grasp tight enough to make Caden's eyes water. Then he shoved Caden's head down while levering his powerful hips up. Caden choked on the big dick and kept on doing so because his master's hold wasn't letting him pull back. Desperate for relief before he passed out or threw up, Caden worked the cock with everything he had. Cum burst into his mouth, gagging him even more. He swallowed furiously and kept trying to pull back until Baker finally let him go.

Caden coughed and wiped his lips with the back of his hand in an attempt to keep cum from dribbling out. He didn't see the slap coming until he was tossed to the floor from the force of it. He lay panting on his side, not daring to look at his master for fear he couldn't keep his hatred off his face. He'd been right, though. The force behind the blow was like being hit by a two-by-four. He didn't even know what he'd done to earn it.

His confusion must have shown.

"You got cum on my pants. I don't like mess." Baker tossed back his drink. "Zipper me back in."

With careful movements, Caden got back on his knees and tucked the man into his underwear and righted his clothes. Then he stayed there staring at…nothing, really. He put an image of the Grahams' island in his head. Pretty colors, gentle breeze. He would have conjured up Tate's face but didn't want to bring him into this miserable tableau.

"Go back to your room. I'll punish you properly later. That tap was just a warm-up so you don't get any ideas about my being soft on you just because of your pretty face and tight ass. I'll teach you how to suck me properly, too. After I fuck your ass," he added with a smirk.

"Yes, Master." Caden slowly got to his feet and did as told. He kept his gaze down while he slipped on the robe and quietly left the room.

He held his tears back. There would be plenty of time when he was alone to let his misery show. Right now, he refused to give this fucker, Chau, or anyone else in this fucking place the satisfaction of seeing how this one encounter had broken Caden already.

* * * *

Tate gave the guy waiting for him a broad smile. "Thanks for hanging tight in this ball-freezing cold, dude." He handed the bike shop owner the purchase price for the Ducati, then peeled off another five hundred dollars as a tip. "I owe you one."

The man took the money and tucked it into his pocket. "Hey, no problems. I don't usually get to sell one of these babies sight unseen. I appreciate the business." He shrugged further into his leather jacket. "It's kind of a bitch out there, man. We had some snow earlier in the day. Not much, but the roads are a little slick in places. Not exactly great riding conditions. Especially farther up the mountain."

"No worries. I've got to be somewhere in a hurry and I've ridden in worse."

The guy smiled. "Yeah, I recognize your name and your face. Seen you race plenty of times on ESPN. You've got like a death wish or something, my man."

Not anymore. He grinned back. "I've heard that a lot. But this time, I have an important appointment to make. Not a thrill ride. Thanks again."

He shook hands with the man and watched him leave before readying himself for the trip to Baker's lair. That was the best way to think of his destination. Baker had always struck him as a kind of Bond villain wannabe. His chalet sat on a mountain side, with acres of land belonging to him, and guards around the perimeter. He was well-protected, just like Tate had been on the island. No one was going to breach the security to steal from him, or whatever it was he thought his risks were. But like on the island, there was a weak spot. Every entryway to the chalet was secure. Except for the rock cliff in the back. No one was crazy enough to try to scale that rock, so they didn't bother to guard it. He knew because Baker had said as much, a brag about how invincible he was.

Yeah, nobody was stupid enough to try to break in on the cliffside, other than Tate, that was. Of course, he was driven by a higher motivation than wanting to abscond with money and Lalique baubles. He wanted the one thing of true value in that place. Caden. That made him willing to take a risk no one else would.

The pack he'd bought in St. Thomas held the warm weather clothing he needed. He put it down and took out what he'd require in order to ride without suffering from frost bite and hypothermia. It was freezing just standing there. The wind from riding the bike would be way worse. As he took out his stuff, he fingered the clothing he'd bought for Caden. He had to make sure his boy was equally protected when he brought him down to safety. With his clothing out, there was room for the extra helmet the bike shop owner had left for him. Then he used a girth hitch to secure the pack to the bike.

He took a moment to steady himself. The ride up didn't worry him. The climb didn't, either. Not more than was necessary to make him alert and cautious. Experience gave him the confidence he would succeed. What terrified him was what he'd find once he reached his destination. Baker had had Caden for a few days now. Images of what the fucker might have been doing to the boy made him sick and furious. Whatever state he was in, Caden would likely need a lot of patience and care. He was brave and resilient, but everyone had their breaking point. Baker had bragged that he always found that spot in everyone he went up against.

Tate was going to see that Caden got all that was necessary to put the experience behind him.

Tate slammed the full-face helmet onto his head and swung onto the bike's seat. It started with a roar. He had to keep the speed down while still at the regional airport. Being early evening, the place wasn't exactly bustling, but he didn't want any trouble or delays. Once he pulled out onto the road, however, he opened up the throttle and raced to his destination.

* * * *

Tate studied the cliff as he changed his heavy biker boots for his climbing shoes. He'd had to hustle through the woods to reach this spot. With the tall, thick fir trees blocking the way, there wasn't much snow to worry about. The crunch of the leaves that had fallen from other types of trees as he jogged his way sounded like fireworks to his worried ears. He'd never been in this area of Baker's land before, yet it wasn't hard to know where to go. The chalet rose into the sky, challenging the trees' dominance of the landscape. As he'd gotten closer, he'd forced himself to slow down, stay low, and watch for any signs of security cameras.

This climb was going to be hellish. Snow and some ice clinging to the rock shone in the moonlight. The only good thing was that there were lots of places for his hands and feet to latch onto. It was going to have to be a free climb. He didn't dare use pitons, ropes and a harness for fear of the sound carrying as he anchored himself along the way. Breaching the Baker compound this way only worked if no one heard him coming. The good thing, he reminded himself, was that it was a one-way trip. He wouldn't have to bring Caden down this way once he found him. There was a simple solution to the problem of Baker owning him. It was just a matter of reaching Caden and convincing him to say the words that would set him free. Baker was an asshole who would think nothing of his goons escorting Tate off the premises, but once he was with the slave, the man would be smart enough not to stop them from leaving.

Every moment he wasted was more time for Caden to be hurt. He switched his cold weather gloves for his climbing ones, stuffed the heavier gloves back into the pack and slipped it on. His shoulder twinged, as did his leg from all the exertion of his travels. Sailing had been the easiest part on his body. Flying hadn't been bad, either. But he'd done a lot of walking to get from one place to another and keeping control of the bike on the slick roads had just added to the strain. As he approached the rock, he shut off the pain and refused to think about how much more he was going to hurt during the climb. It simply didn't matter. Only Caden did.

He stood at the bottom of the cliff and sized up a path to the top as much as he could see from the ground. He went over it again a few times so that he wouldn't have to figure it out as he went. That was key to a good climb. He took a deep breath and let it out slowly, then grabbed his first hold. It was tough going at first, a hand and a foot slipping a few heart-stopping times. But there were more dry holds as he got farther up, and the rock face itself was craggy. He didn't have to strain too much on either side to pull himself up. He knew better than to look too far beyond the few feet above him. If he did, it would be easy to become anxious to speed his progress. That could be dangerous. And while he often looked down when he climbed for the thrill of it, he didn't this time. He didn't have the time to indulge and he rather feared that now that he had a reason to live, he might not like looking way, way down anymore.

He stayed focused, concentrating on the here and now, taking on each leg of the journey as it came. It meant putting aside thoughts of Caden and communing with the rock as he'd learned to do. He listened to it and changed his path when it warned him to. When pain tried to intrude on his thoughts, he shoved it down. Now was not the time to give into the demands of his booboos. Nothing was going to break or tear under the strain. He was past that worry. There was no seat at the table for discomfort. He could soak in a hot tub later and even down a pill. But not now.

He swallowed a grunt as he hauled himself up. He knew how to climb, was better than most, and had done it for fun dozens of times and under worse conditions. This journey, however, wasn't for the thrill of the risk or out of a deep-seated need to flip off his parents. This climb had a noble goal and it was going to take all of his skill and experience to achieve it.

* * * *

"Did you use the enema while in the shower?" Chau asked the question with his usual combination of disinterest and disdain. The man clearly didn't like playing the role of madam for Baker's whore. Although he also seemed to have some kind of perverse interest in Caden's plight, as well.

Pervert. Asshole.

It helped to think of them all with the same contempt they showed him.

"Yes," he bit out. "I'm not a child. I can follow orders and know how to clean myself."

For a moment, he thought Chau was going to hit him. But no, that was Baker's privilege. Caden's cheek still stung from the hard slap and there was a red mark where the contact had occurred. He supposed that mild hurt was going to be a fond memory after this coming night. Caden stood still while the house manager gave him the once-over to make sure he met the master's requirements. The man went so far as to spread Caden's ass cheeks for a peek at his hole. The humiliation was nothing. He could stand it. He had no choice.

Chau stepped around to face him and sneered. "You look almost like a child, so that's good enough for Mr. Baker."

Learning that his new master was the worst kind of pervert wasn't surprising. The slave agent had remarked that his boyish face would appeal to a lot of men. He hadn't given it much thought then and it hardly mattered because he was, after all, an adult. The idea of being some pedophile's legal fantasy still made his stomach roil. Although maybe that meant the man wouldn't keep him for the full ten years. Not that such a thought should be comforting. The people who bought debt slaves were proving to be even worse than he could have imagined. No one Baker sold him on to would be an improvement, he was sure.

Chau moved toward the door. "He is on a business call. Stay here until he summons you. I expect by tomorrow morning you'll have a more respectful mouth." With that last shot, the man left the room.

Alone, Caden tried to settle his nerves by returning to his bed and picking up his book. Remaining still proved impossible, however. He stood again and went to the small window in his tiny room. It was designed for a servant—and not one very high up on the household scale at that. It did have an attached bathroom, but that was only so that he could keep himself in the shape Baker expected him to be at all times. He tugged open the blinds and peered into the dark forest. It was probably considered a bad view for a bedroom, yet he liked it. If he stared out into the distance, he could imagine himself somewhere else. Anywhere else.

Not the Grahams' island, though. This place was far too different for that fantasy and it had been a mistake to even try to conjure it. Which was all to the good. He needed to forget about that brief period in his life. It was over. He'd probably never see Tate again, and what difference did it make? It wasn't as if the guy was going to greet him like an old friend. For a brief time, they'd been master and slave, sort of friends and fuck buddies. Nothing more, no matter what his heart was telling him. Harding had been right. This wasn't some fairytale where the downtrodden servant got swept up by the handsome prince. He was nothing more than a sex toy and one that could be treated anyway his owner liked. He could never terminate his contract and put himself in a worse financial position. Debtor's prison hadn't been brought back, but defrauding creditors was a crime, making prison an easy answer to people like him. This way still seemed like the better choice. He wouldn't last a second in a place like that without hooking up with some big, bad killer. Someone like Baker, really, only with less money and no freedom.

None of his choices were good ones. Despair wrapped around him.

The window was only latched. The room hadn't been turned into a real prison. Nothing would stop him from raising the sash and climbing onto the sill. He was three stories up and that kind of fall would almost certainly kill him. His hand hovered over the latch of its own volition. He had to snatch it back and step away. That wasn't the answer. No matter what happened, he could survive. Maybe, if he was really good and lucky, he could have access to the internet and follow Tate's newest adventures. While he hoped his former master wouldn't go back to risking his life, it would be really nice to watch him playing some kind of sport. Maybe see him at a movie premiere or other glamorous event with a gorgeous man on his arm. It would hurt, but it was what Tate deserved — happiness with someone worthy of him.

The door opening startled him.

Chau was there, pointing for him to leave. Caden threw on his robe and walked past the man with as much dignity as he could muster. The master's suite was on the floor below. Caden followed the house manager down the back staircase, then the hall, and stepped inside when he opened a door. He found himself inside a sitting room filled with the same dark wood and leather that the study had been decorated in. It was bleak more than masculine.

"Get your ass in here!"

Baker's voice boomed from the bedroom beyond. Caden only hesitated a moment before complying. It was dimly lit, like a cave or a dungeon, although he hardly noticed the décor because Baker's large, naked body grabbed his attention immediately. He stumbled a bit at the sight. Out of his clothes, the man appeared even bigger and more muscular, with only a slightly rounded belly that men his age couldn't quite avoid no matter how much time they spent in a gym. He wouldn't have minded under different circumstances. Ones where he wasn't dreading what was to come. Baker's massive dick was on full display, jutting out from a hairy groin, telegraphing just how rough the night, and every one after it, was going to be. Caden couldn't help cringe at the sight of it.

Baker chuckled and palmed the shaft. "I'm a big man. You are going to both love and hate this. Take off that robe, and don't make me have to tell you that again. In my presence, you will always be on display. Understand?"

"Yes, Master." Caden once more stripped himself naked to the hungry eyes of someone who owned him.

Baker walked over to a low table that held a thick belt, a wooden paddle and a suede flogger with balls at the end of each tail. He gestured toward them. "Choose."

Caden blinked hard a few times. "I'm sorry?"

"This first time, I'm letting you pick what I'm going to beat you with. Choose." His voice held a hard edge to it.

Caden felt as if he were in a waking nightmare as he approached the table. He liked rough sex but hadn't gone into the BDSM scene because he didn't think he'd like the experience of punishment. Or of prolonged pain. Not that it mattered. Despite the contract he'd signed, he wasn't about to engage in a consensual scene. He'd merely agreed to acquiesce to his master's demands no matter what he himself wanted. Baker was never going to stop doing whatever he wanted simply because Caden pineappled him. The man's impatience was obvious, so Caden went with what he thought might hurt the least and pointed to the belt.

Baker chuckled as he picked up the thick strap and folded the ends together. He snapped the leather with a loud crack that made Caden jump. "Excellent choice. You won't be able to sit for a few days. Not comfortably, anyway. Especially as tonight, remember, is about punishment, nor merely a warmup for sex." He pointed to the bed. "Bend over the side."

Blinking back sudden tears, Caden obeyed. As he laid his head onto the silky duvet, he closed his eyes and pictured the island despite his resolve not to. He lacked the strength to endure without it and needed something lovely to hang onto. Not Tate, though. He wasn't going to bring him into this degrading experience even in his imagination. Instead, he saw the ocean sparkling in the distance, smelled the perfume of the riotously colored flowers and heard the exotic bird song that seemed never ending there. This was going to be his happy place, where he'd go each and every time he was forced to submit to what he didn't want.

He could only hope it would be enough.

* * * *

Tate forced himself to rest. The climb had been a killer and served to remind him at a screaming decibel that he wasn't a hundred percent yet. His leg shook from the exertion of pushing himself up and his collarbone ached like a bitch from all the pulling his hand had done. He ignored them both. Once he'd caught his wind, he'd finish the journey with one more obstacle to scale. The pain could wait to be soothed away and if he was lucky, he'd have Caden to help him do so. *No. Not luck. I command my own fate.* Yeah, he left nothing to chance. So long as he was prepared and balled his way through any hurdles, he won. That's what life over the last few years of pushing the limits of his body and skill had taught him. He was going to succeed because he knew what he was doing. And he also understood that the only easy day was yesterday. To expect anything else was a waste of effort. Everything he'd done since losing Jimmy had led him to this point. He was ready for anything that Baker might throw at him, including this next phase of getting into the house.

The brief rest served the additional purpose of giving him time to study the movements of the guards. He could see one each patrolling on either side of the yard, meandering around the side, then disappearing toward the front. They both gave cursory glances at the back, but neither of them bothered to make a full sweep. No one would be motivated to risk the climb. Or so they assumed, because this was New York, after all, not a war zone. There would be too much risk for too little monetary reward. And Baker wasn't the president or anything, merely a rich man making sure his stuff didn't get stolen. No one had an ideological purpose in breaching the place this way. Except for Tate. Love might not be the same thing as a cause, but it was a damn good motivator. The guards only carried side-arms, too, not the automatic weapons used by the island guards. There were no pirates in the Hudson Valley. Not that he intended to battle any of them.

Having recovered his wind and timed the movements of the guards, Tate launched out of his hiding place to streak across the lawn over to the pool house. The building gave him a shadowy place to hide while he scouted out the main house. He gave only a brief look at the windows on the first floor. Not much was happening there. A maid passed by on her way to what he assumed was the kitchen. Knowing Baker would be nowhere near the servants' area, he shifted his gaze to the second floor and in particular the long balcony smack in the middle. A row of tall windows gave him a perfect view into what had to be Baker's bedroom. Confirmation came from the man himself as he strolled past. From what Tate could see, Baker was naked. His heart tripped at the knowledge that Caden was likely already there, too, forced to cater to the bastard's needs.

He clenched his fingers with the urge to smash Baker's face. But that wasn't going to help Caden. Tate had to keep his wits about him. He was almost there, almost at Caden's side. All he had to do was keep his shit together for a little longer. He scanned the yard for a glimpse of the guards and waited until they made their turn back to the front before racing to the bushes lined against the chalet. They were covered in burlap to protect them from the harsh winter, so they were skinnier than he would have liked to act as a shield. But he was in all black and the night sky had decided to lend him a hand by having clouds roll in to block most of the moonlight.

He studied the outside of the house as he had the cliff face. This was going to be a hell of a different climb than the cliff. Drain pipes and their clamps provide the perfect holds and no snow or ice covered any of it that he could see. He straightened to test one and, finding it secure, started his journey up to the balcony.

It was a piece of cake compared to the cliffside. His not-fully recovered injuries begged to differ. He ignored the pleading for him to stop, focusing on the relief he'd soon be feeling at finding Caden. He would take him out of this gilded hellhole and back home to his townhouse in Boston. He'd divorce himself from his parents once and for all. Caden would be free and Tate would make sure he didn't have to worry about anything. They could begin a real relationship, maybe get married, have kids. He paused mid-climb for a second to marvel at how he was already planning a new life. It was exhilarating and terrifying at the same time, if only because he'd never discussed anything so detailed with Caden. They'd shied away from thinking very far in the future and allowed themselves to be too focused on enjoying their time together to consider where their lives might be going. Maybe given the choice, Caden wouldn't want him anymore.

The mere thought of Caden not wanting him filled his heart with dread. Although it had been mere weeks since the boy had first come into his life, he realized he couldn't imagine a future without him. He also couldn't imagine imposing his will on him. It wouldn't mean anything if he set him free only to demand he stay with him out of gratitude. The boy would need space, probably, time to figure out what he wanted out of life. Tate could be patient. He would have to be, because it was the fair thing to do. He wasn't his parents or Baker. Sure, it would crush his heart if he lost Caden, but that didn't change the fact that this was the right thing to do.

A scream from above startled him out of reflection. With a growl, he scrambled up the pipe, grabbed the railing of the terrace and hoisted himself onto it. He landed in a crouch and wiggled out of the pack to be unencumbered as he dashed for the sliding doors. He would have thrown himself through the glass as if in a bad action movie if necessary. Fortunately, his head was still in the game and he checked to see if they were unlocked. And they were. He shoved them open and launched into Baker's bedroom. The sight that greeted him had him howling. His stride didn't break as he ran to Baker and tore the belt out of his hand just as the asshole was about to land another blow on Caden's ass.

"Get away from him, fucker!" He shoved the man back and stood between him and Caden.

"What the hell are you doing here, Tate?" Baker's face was turning red as he yelled out the question.

"Rescuing Caden." He didn't dare take his eyes off Baker, yet held out his free hand behind him. "It's okay, baby. Can you stand up?"

A second later, a hand slid into his. "I'm okay." Caden's voice was shaky, though. "He only got off one blow. I, ah, didn't even have a chance to pineapple him." The boy gave a weak laugh as he moved to cling to Tate's arm.

Tate bared his teeth at Baker. "He's the one who's going to have to say pineapple. Not that it will do him any good."

Baker threw up one arm even as he lurched to press the call button by his bed. "What the fuck are you talking about? I bought this slut from your parents. He doesn't need *rescuing*. He's mine. I can do whatever I like with him."

"That's where you're wrong, asshole." Tate flicked his gaze at the man's shriveling erection. "I haven't seen that part of you since you flashed me in the locker room at the club. What was I, fifteen at the time? You sick puppy. I bet you didn't even ask Caden if he got off on this kind of pain."

"He's my slave. I don't have to ask his permission for anything, or care what he likes or doesn't like. I shouldn't have to explain that to you. What are you, brain-damaged or something? How hard did you hit your head anyway to think you can break into my home and tell me what to do with what's mine? I'm calling your parents to come get you."

"They have nothing to say about this." Tate didn't have a chance to explain anything to Caden before the door burst open and two guards came in.

Tate threw down the belt so that they wouldn't have a reason to get trigger happy. Then took Caden fully into his arms and rubbed his hand down his arm to soothe them both.

"Get him out of here," Baker ordered, his finger pointing at Tate.

"Don't worry, we're leaving."

Baker turned his hateful gaze on Tate. "You really are brain-damaged. I said I'd bought the boy from your parents. You go. He stays."

Tate wasted no more time. He turned Caden in order to look him in the eye. "All you have to do to leave with me is terminate the contract. It only takes words, baby. Tell him you're terminating your contract. The law says you can break it at any time just by saying so. It's the one good part of the despicable rules."

Caden stared back at him with tears in his eyes. "You know I can't."

"Of course you can." Tate mentally slapped himself for failing to tell him everything. "I'll cover your debts and the break-up penalty. You'll walk out of here free of any burden."

"I can't ask you to do that."

Tate tamped down his impatience. The guards were looking like they were going to head over to them. "You're not. This is all my idea. I want to do it. I *have* to do it." He moistened his lips, hating the setting in which he was going to be forced to declare his feelings. "I love you."

Caden blinked back tears. "Really?"

Tate grinned. "Yeah. And you know, we won't be able to return to the island because I'm going to tell my horrid parents to go pound sand. But I have a nice townhouse in Boston. And an apartment in London, and one in Paris. None of them are paradise. I think you'll like them anyway. That is, if you want to stay with me," he forced himself to say. "That's not part of any deal. I'm clearing your debt regardless." His heart nearly froze as he waited for an answer.

Caden barked out a laugh. "You think I don't want to be with you? There's nowhere I'd rather be because I love you too."

"Jesus." Baker snorted. "This is all very touching…"

Caden turned to the man. "Mr. Baker, I am terminating my debt contract with you. Go fuck yourself. Your dick is probably long enough to reach your ass, but that's the only thing you've got to brag about. Oh, and I'm twenty, by the way. Sorry if that shatters any illusions you've built up in your horrible, sick, little mind."

Baker sputtered. "Why…you…"

The guards took a few steps their way without Baker telling them to. They probably weren't very bright and didn't understand what was happening, how their employer had already lost. At least Tate hoped so. Maybe Baker wasn't beyond acting like a Bond villain after all.

"Don't be an idiot, Baker," Tate warned. "Although you get away with a lot of shit, you're always careful not to cross any obvious lines. If you don't let us go peacefully, I'm going to put up one hell of a fight." He flicked his gaze at the guards. "You know I compete in mixed martial arts. I'm pretty sure I can mess up your boys. And letting them shoot me would be a really dumb move. My parents can bury you if they want, and as much as they are disappointed in me, they close ranks when the outside threatens the family. Plus, you know…I'd call the police. Unless you intend to bury me in a shallow grave in the Poconos?"

It only took a moment for Baker to make the right decision. He waved the guards to stand down. "Get out, then. No slut's worth this trouble."

Tate relaxed a fraction. He wouldn't truly feel relieved until he was flying Caden back to Boston. "You're wrong on two counts. Caden is not a slut, and he's worth any amount of trouble."

He moved away from the bed and over to the balcony. "I have some clothes for Caden in my pack outside. He needs to get dressed. And then...we're going to require a ride down to where my bike is parked. I'm sure one of your boys will be happy to give us a lift."

He shot Baker a triumphant smile and took pleasure in seeing the old man's dick shrink completely.

Chapter Ten

Caden didn't have time to feel nervous or give into the need to break down entirely and sob like a baby. Not with Baker's goons still nearby. These two were particularly mad about having been stuck with the job of driving way down the mountain road to where Tate had stashed his ginormous motorcycle. Their orders were to make sure they left for good, and something told him that these assholes might be inclined to use those guns strapped to their waist and claim self-defense now that they were no longer in Baker's home.

Tate didn't act like he was nervous, but he hadn't wasted any time helping Caden into a thick leather jacket, tugging on warm gloves, and placing a helmet on his head before doing the same for himself.

"Hold on tight," he said as Caden slung his leg over the wide seat. "And don't worry. I've got you, baby."

Caden was happy to hug onto the man's waist with arms that continued to feel like jelly. So much had happened in the last couple of hours, he was a mess of emotions and felt as if he'd run a marathon. It was still hard to process how his life had turned drastically around in the blink of an eye. One moment, he'd been dealing with the pain of being belted across the ass, and the next, he'd been in Tate's strong, warm embrace. It was hard to accept that he was free. But he trusted Tate and more, loved him. Surprisingly, the guy loved him back. It was like a dream. A good one, but also something that could evaporate in the cold light of day.

He snuggled closer to his man as they roared off down the road. His ass was a bit tender from just the one blow. Baker had a heavy hand. How much worse would he be feeling after God only knew the number of blows the bastard intended to inflict before fucking him with his monster dick? He shuddered at the thought of the damage that could have been done to him.

"Sorry. I know it's cold." Tate shouted over the loud engine. "I'm going to stop for the rest of the night at a motel."

Caden pressed his head against the man's back. Let him think it was the icy wind that had made him shiver and not the fright of the near miss back in Baker's house. Tate had to be in great pain after everything he'd done, but he was as solid as the rock mountains surrounding them. Nothing quivered under Caden's clasp.

When they reached a small town, asleep for the night, Tate dropped his speed and the noise of their passing through. That was the kind of man he was — kind and considerate even to strangers. The raging asshole that he'd first appeared to be had merely been by-products of his pain, misery and probably fear of what his life had become. Caden needed healing from his brief experience as a slave, but Tate had some long-term trauma to work through. He wanted to be there for him as Tate had been for him in his time of need.

There was a bog-standard motel on the other side of the town. It was not the kind of place either of them was used to frequenting. There was a charm to it, though, and it felt vaguely naughty to rent a room for the night with Tate paying in cash. The sleepy desk clerk perked right up when Tate handed him an extra hundred dollars for the inconvenience.

As they walked to their room, Caden decided it was time to find out exactly what had happened since Harding had dragged him off the island.

"Are you worried about being traced?"

Tate looked up from where he worked the old-fashioned key into the door. "Hmm?" He shoved it open to a small, clean room.

"You paid with cash, so I figured we're, like, on the run. Or something." Caden shut the door, removed his jacket and tossed it, his gloves and his helmet on a chair.

Tate chuckled. "Oh. No, baby. I'm not. We're not. I just couldn't find my wallet in the safe on the island so have been making do with cash."

Caden wasn't able to ask another question because Tate pulled him in for a sweet kiss.

Tate pressed his forehead against Caden's when he broke it off far too soon. "I wasn't sure what shape I would find you in, but I was really scared that Baker would hurt you badly before I got there. It took forever for me to reach you."

Caden took over the role of caretaker because Tate obviously needed comfort. "Baker only arrived today. I've been mostly bored. And scared," he admitted. If they were going to have any kind of life together, they had to be honest with each other.

"Oh, baby. So was I." Tate pulled him into a tight hug. "When I woke up and found out what had happened, I thought I was going to lose my mind. I'm sorry I didn't protect you."

Caden ran his palm up his man's back. "There was nothing you could have done. I was just glad they knocked you out before taking me away. I wouldn't have wanted you to get hurt." He pulled back and scrutinized Tate. "Your injuries must be killing you."

Tate rolled his shoulder. "Not badly. The climb was tough, I admit. A hot shower should help." He gave him a smoldering look. "Let's both take one." He removed his jacket and tossed them on a chair with Caden's stuff.

"Wait, what?" Caden asked as Tate took him by the hand and dragged him to the bathroom. "You climbed something? I mean, just up to the balcony, right?"

"That plus the cliffside on the back of Baker's property. It was the only way to get in without being detected." Tate grabbed the hem of the sweater he'd brought for him and tugged it over his head.

When his face was free, Caden popped his eyes. "You rock climbed?" Glancing down, he noticed for the first time that Tate was wearing weird shoes. "In those?"

"Well, yeah. And with these." He held up his hands and stripped off his thin gloves. "I had warmer gloves in the pack, so leaving that behind with Baker was dumb. I was in such a hurry to get you out of there, I wasn't thinking clearly. And I had to leave my biker boots in the woods. Too bulky to carry on my back." He shrugged. "I'll see about buying more before we head to the airport."

Tate knelt to remove Caden's sneakers, then undid his jeans. His cock sprung out, because of course being this close to his lover aroused him.

"Hmm. I'm glad I forgot to bring you underwear." Tate licked a stripe up the shaft, making it twitch.

Caden put his hand on Tate's head, mostly to steady himself. "Wait. We need to talk."

"I'd really rather not." A sound like a growl passed his lips as he stared at the red spot on Caden's ass. "I might go back and beat Baker to a pulp before we leave." He pressed a gentle kiss on the mark before standing. "Let's get that shower started."

Before he could formulate a response, Caden landed under the shower with blessedly hot water pounding out and washing away the memories of his time with Baker. Better yet, Tate joined him quickly, his cock as hard as Caden's. No surprise there. Once they'd moved past their mutual resentment, the attraction had been a potent thing. He didn't think he would ever not want this man. And he could let go of his questions for a little while and enjoy his new freedom.

Tate dropped to his knees and sucked Caden's dick in his mouth almost to the root. He wanted to object to the stress it had to be causing Tate's leg to kneel on the tile. Although the man had climbed an icy cliff to reach him, so maybe he didn't need to worry too much. Tate swallowed around Caden's shaft, sending sparks right to his balls. With a groan, he braced against the wall and locked his knees. He came in a blinding rush that would have caused him to slide down to the bottom of the shower if Tate hadn't caught him in his strong embrace.

The kiss this time was bold, Tate's tongue sweeping through Caden's mouth. He could taste his own cum and wanted to reciprocate the blow job to mingle their flavors. Tate's hold was too strong for him to break free, so he made do with shoving his hand between their bodies and grabbing the guy's cock. A few awkward jerks and Tate was groaning down his throat as cum splashed over them both.

Tate broke the kiss and panted into his ear. "I want to fuck you more than I want my next breath, but we're going to wait. We both need rest and I don't want to hurt you."

"Because of the tender spot on my ass? It's nothing."

"Yes, because of that, and it's not nothing. Neither is this." Tate touched Caden's cheek. "He hit you in the face, too, didn't he?"

"Oh." He'd forgotten about the slap. It had hardly left a mark. Leave it to Tate to notice.

"That's nothing, too. You're all that matters, being here and wanting me. Everything else is just noise. Let's block it out for tonight."

Tate nodded. "Okay. I mean it about the rest, though. I don't think…" Tate leaned heavily on him.

"Oh shit!" Alarm shot through Caden. Grabbing Tate under the arms, he helped him out of the shower and over to the bed. "You've overdone it, idiot!" He raced to get a towel to dry him off.

Tate groaned, and not in a good way. "Worth it."

Caden rubbed him down, careful of the leg and chest area. "When was the last time you slept?"

"I dunno. What day is it? Not since I woke to find you gone, anyway."

"God damn! Are you training to become a Navy SEAL or something? You didn't have to chase after me so quickly."

Tate grabbed his wrist with surprising strength. "Every second you were with that asshole was a risk to you. I couldn't bear it."

Caden rolled his eyes. "He wasn't going to kill me."

"He was going to hurt you. He did hurt you. I was scared, baby."

Touched at the concern he saw in his lover's eyes, Caden had to swallow past a lump in his throat. "My hero. Now, get some sleep." He wrangled Tate under the covers.

"You'll sleep with me?"

"Of course. There's only one bed and I'm done with sleeping on the floor next to you."

He padded back to the bathroom to dry himself off and hang the wet towels. When he returned, Tate was already out. Feeling lighthearted for the first time in months, Caden slipped between the sheets and followed him down.

* * * *

Tate woke achy all over. Even those parts of his body that hadn't been injured hurt like a bitch. He'd been too out of shape for what he'd done, yet it had been worth it. Caden was here, by his side, safe and sound. Ignoring everything else, he concentrated on the part of him that hurt in a good way and was also hard. The source of his arousal was lying snug against his side. Caden's warm breath teased his shoulder and his soft hand lay on his stomach, just above where his cock hovered. He rolled onto his side and rubbed against Caden's hip.

The boy grinned with his eyes closed. "You can't possibly feel up to this. Not after the few days you've had."

Tate bucked his hips. "My dick and I beg to differ."

Opening his eyes, Caden propped up on his elbows. "Tell me what you have planned for the day."

Tate frowned. He wasn't sure where this was going but he answered anyway because he would do anything for Caden. "Well, first we'll go get breakfast. Then we'll go to the regional airport where I have a rented plane waiting and we'll fly to Boston. Get lunch. Go to my townhouse. Fuck like bunnies. Eat dinner. And make a plan for the rest of our lives." A sudden fear shot through him. "That is, if you want to be with me. I don't want you to feel obligated." He lowered his gaze. "Last night was pretty intense. I'll understand if you said things you might feel differently about this morning."

Caden grunted. "Don't be stupid. I fell in love with you when you were still my master. Of course I want to spend the rest of my life with you. And that's not my fear of Baker or my gratitude for my rescue talking. You need to believe what I say, Tate."

Relief made him sigh. "Thank God. Anyway, that's what I figured we'd do today. Do you have other ideas? Whatever you want, I'll give you."

Caden didn't answer right away. Instead, he sat up and turned to kneel facing him. His dick was also hard. "I don't. Have anything I'd rather do than just as you laid out. I approve of your itinerary. But here's the thing. Do you think I have the ability to ride a motorcycle and fly a plane?"

"I didn't think so. Can you?"

Caden shook his head. "Not in a million years. Which means that if we are going to get back to Boston today, you need to be fit enough to do so."

Tate grabbed Caden's shaft and squeezed. "Believe me, baby, I'm up for it."

"Uh, huh. Let's not take any chances. We need you to conserve your energy."

With Tate still gripping his cock, Caden threw a leg over Tate's thighs and took his dick into an equally tight grip.

Tate moaned and bucked into the hold. Only once, though. He was really primed and didn't want to come too soon. "Mutual masturbation?" Not what he had in mind, but not unwelcome.

Caden shook his head before bending over and licking Tate's shaft. The softness of the tongue bath was surprisingly electrifying. It made it too awkward for him to keep hold of Caden's dick, however. He had to let go and half closed his eyes. He wanted to watch as well as feel as Caden gobbled him down. Except the boy had yet another idea, and gave no warning before he positioned Tate's cock between his ass cheeks and sat all the way down.

"Jesus!" Tate grabbed the boy by his waist to try to lift him off. "Baby, we don't have lube. You're hurting yourself."

Caden shook his head again and gazed down at him with hooded eyelids. "I like this kind of pain. You know that. It's not the same as Baker," he added before Tate could raise the point. "This is a choice I'm making and I'm going to do all the work. You only have to lie back and take it."

Trusting Caden to know his own mind and body, Tate relaxed and did as he was told.

Caden surprisingly relished the power that came from being in charge and controlling their love-making. He hadn't been in the position with anyone frequently, and didn't want to be in the driver's seat often, yet he took pride as well as pleasure in leading his lover in chasing a climax. The initial burn of being breached without any proper lubrication or preparation had set his whole body on fire, sending shivers of delight and pain throughout him. He sat fully seated on Tate for a few seconds to allow his channel to adjust to the invasion, staring into the man's eyes, trying to convey his love wordlessly.

Tate's chest rose and fell on quick breaths and his blown pupils displayed his arousal. Being ridden excited the typically dominant guy. Caden would have to tuck that information away for future use. It would be fun to reverse roles once in a while, given that they both enjoyed it, but only in bed. He craved having a man take care of him and now he knew that it didn't take an older lover to achieve that dynamic. Remembering how Tate had raced to his side to save him, taking huge risks doing so, made his heart swell with emotion. He had to tell him how he felt.

Caden lifted up a bit before sliding down again on the hot cock inside him. He and Tate both moaned with the intensity of the pleasure.

He did it again. "Your dick fills me as no one else's ever has."

Tate grinned before grabbing Caden's shaft. "I like this view." He squeezed hard enough to force out another groan. "I want to see you come all over my fingers." He swiped his thumbnail through the slit. "Then I'm going to lick it off."

Caden stuttered out a breath and picked up the pace, posting on Tate's cock. "I want to stay with you, Tate. Forever. I'm not going to change my mind about that. This isn't just a 'let's be boyfriends' thing, either. I'm fully committed to you. To us."

Tate jerked him with matching speed. "Good because that's what I want, too. I didn't free you only to trap you for myself. It's your choice, Caden. Entirely. Please believe that. And I'm also looking for forever."

Caden shook his head. "Whatever choice I had flew away from the moment I saw you." He chuckled a bit as he clenched on the upstroke. "I didn't realize it then, but my feelings for you became crystal clear as Harding dragged me away. I didn't want to leave you. I never will."

Tate clutched Caden's knee with his free hand. "You don't have to worry about anyone taking you against your will ever again. I'll take good care of you. We'll buy our own island if you want."

Caden gnawed at his lower lip as the orgasm grew. "Maybe someday. I had some time to think while I waited for Baker to come home, spun some fantasies, actually, that have crystalized really just in this moment. I want to go back to college and eventually go onto law school. I didn't take more than a few college level courses in easy topics before dropping out, so it will take a long time for me to get my degree. It's worth the effort, though. Someone has to fight these horrid debt slave laws." He stared intently into his lover's eyes. "I want to make a difference in the world."

Tate held his gaze and arched into his ass. "That's a great idea. As I made my way to you, I also had time to consider my life. What do you think of my establishing a green energy company?"

Caden panted as he picked up speed, bearing down on Tate's cock with each movement up and down. "Sounds like a great idea."

Tate flicked his wrist as his fingers tore up and down Caden's shaft. "It will really piss my parents off for me to try to make their oil pumping obsolete." He groaned. "Fast, baby, faster. Yeah, like that. And I want to get married."

Caden pumped his hips, his thighs beginning to burn from the effort. "Oh yeah. Me too. I'll take your name and I want two kids with an option for a third."

"Perfect." Tate grunted. "Christ, your ass is like a vise. I'm not going to last much longer."

The tingle in his balls warned Caden he was close to coming. "Good, I don't want you to." He pushed on Tate's chest to leverage himself for more speed.

Tate gritted his teeth. "We'll name the first child Beckett. Even if it's a girl. I mean, how cute is Becky for a nickname?"

"You don't want to call them James after your brother? That can work for a girl, too. Jamie."

"We'll use that the second time around."

Caden tried to respond, but the climax tore through him. No longer able to keep his eyes open, he threw back his head and gripped Tate's cock as hard as he could as the waves of pleasure rocketed through him. Warmth splashed inside him just as Tate's howl filled the room. They both shuddered and bucked, and when the high of the orgasm started to subside, Caden fell on top of his lover and melted against him.

Tate freed his hand from where it was squished between them, then cupped Caden's ass with both hands.

He buried his face into Caden's neck. "I love you."

Caden snuggled closer. "I'll never grow tired of hearing that."

"Good. I'll be sure to say it every day for the rest of our lives."

A worry that had been tickling the back of his mind pushed its way forward. "I need you to promise me something else, though, that you won't like."

Tate lifted Caden's head so that they were face-to-face, close enough that their noses practically touched. "If it's something that is important to you, I won't hesitate."

"Okay." Caden licked his lips, screwing up the courage to speak his mind. "I need you to give up taking risks. No more extreme sports…at least, not so many. No climbing Mount Everest, okay? I don't want you to die," he couldn't help adding with a hitch to his voice.

"Oh, baby." Tate kissed him sweetly. "With you in my life, I have every reason to keep myself safe. And I don't have to give up the sports I love entirely to ease your mind, right? I don't need triple black diamond slopes to go skiing. If I want to be on the water, I can sail instead of racing speed boats."

Caden's heart lightened. "That's right. I'll even join you." He frowned as the import of Tate's words sunk in. "You want to sail again?"

Tate nodded. "Yeah, it's time. Sailing was the only way off the island, so I had to get over my fears if I was going to rescue you. But it also allowed me to rekindle my love of it without being haunted by Jimmy's death."

He grinned. "This is going to work out, isn't it?"

"Of course." Tate pulled him in for another kiss, longer this time, yet no less sweet.

When they broke apart, Caden frowned. "I think you got cum in my hair."

"Sorry about that. We'll just have to take a shower. Together. Later."

With that, Tate flipped Caden on his back. His cock hadn't entirely slipped free from Caden's ass, so Tate had no trouble thrusting it back in. This time, it was Caden's turn to lie back and let his lover do the work.

Epilogue

"Mom? Dad? What a pleasant surprise." Tate grinned into his parents' furious faces. "Come on in." He stepped aside so that they could enter his townhouse.

They walked in wordlessly, practically vibrating in an effort not to make a scene where someone outside could witness it. Shutting the door, he gestured for them to continue into the front drawing room.

"Won't you have a seat?"

He kept up his cheerful demeanor even though he was royally pissed at them still and felt like crap having arrived home the night before after a grueling trip back from his rescue of Caden. He wouldn't let his fatigue and discomfort show, however. He was damned if he'd give them the satisfaction.

He passed them to sit on the only comfortable chair in the room. "I haven't had time to restaff the place so I can't offer you any refreshments."

His mother shot him a waspish look as she and his father sat stiffly on the sofa. "Why don't you have your slave do it?"

Tate gave them a wide-eyed look of confusion. "I don't have one."

"Don't be obtuse," his mother said with a huff. "Gordon called us last night. He was furious that you dared to take the boy from him."

Tate dropped his grin. "Oh, you mean Caden. Didn't Baker tell you? He's not a slave anymore. In fact, he's my fiancé."

His father scoffed. "Don't be ridiculous. You can't mean to marry that slut."

Tate let his anger show for a moment before relaxing again. "If you're going to insult the man I love, you can get the hell out."

Both of his parents bristled, but before they could spew whatever poison was brewing inside them, Caden walked in. Damn, Tate had thought he was still asleep.

"Don't be too hard on the poor man, Tate. I'm sure he's disappointed he never had a chance to fuck me himself." Caden shot the couple a sweet smile before perching on the arm of Tate's chair.

Tate made a point of grabbing him by the waist and tumbling him onto his lap. "Good point, baby. He won't touch you now, though. No one will except me." He pecked the boy on the lips before turning his attention back to his parents. "Congratulate us, Mom and Dad, we're planning on a June wedding."

His mother waved that announcement away as if it were a bothersome fly. "Don't be ridiculous. You can't marry this...*boy*."

"Oh, but I am, *Mommy Dearest*. I'd do it today if he'd let me. He wants to do it right. Invitations to friends and relatives, a reception. You know, the whole nine yards, and I am helpless to deny him because I love him. I'd say you understand, except I'm sure you don't."

His mother straightened an already straight back. "We will not attend such a farce."

"That's okay. We haven't drawn up the guest list yet, but I'm pretty sure we weren't intending to invite you. Isn't that right, babe?"

Caden curled into him. "Sadly yes. I don't want a reminder that you sold me to a sadistic asshole instead of letting me stay with Tate. I was taking him as he was, you know, and feeling lucky to have found myself being a slave to someone I loved. You did what you did out of spite." Caden's tone had taken a hard edge.

Tate was enormously proud of him. It took real courage to face down the people who had bought and sold you like an object.

"We'll cut you off," his father said. "You'll be fired from all of your company positions."

"Gee, Dad, you mean I can no longer do those jobs I hated anyway? I'll just have to use my inheritance to create one I like better."

"Huh! Pocket change. We'll see how long it lasts to fund your crazy hobbies."

Tate ran his hand up and down Caden's arm, finding the silky skin soothing as he formulated a reply. He was no longer interested in baiting these people.

"When Jimmy died, my world fell apart. His death left a hole in me that you not only didn't try to heal, but you made bigger. I understand that he was your favorite, that I was only ever intended to be a back-up.

Couldn't you have even tried to hide your disappointment that he died instead of me? Did you have to make it so obvious that you had to make do with me?"

Caden snuggled closer and rubbed the back of Tate's neck. The sweet gesture helped calm him and remind him of what he'd gained. His life was no longer bleak.

His mother dismissed his criticism. "You always were too sensitive. So what if you weren't our first choice to take the reins and secure our legacy. We gave you a chance, did we not? We still are." She sneered at Caden. "For once in your life, make a sensible decision. Get rid of this trash and all will be forgiven."

Tate's patience had found its limit. He slowly rose, setting Caden on his feet.

"You can leave now."

"We aren't finished," his father declared, sitting back as if settling in.

Tate disentangled himself from Caden's embrace. "Yes, you are." He took a step forward, ready to toss his parents out bodily if necessary.

Caden reached for him. "Let them stay. We'll go out and get some breakfast, then go grocery shopping. Your cupboards are literally bare. Please." That last word was breathed into his ear in a barely audible voice.

Just like that, Tate's anger deflated once more. "What a great idea, baby." He smirked at his parents. "I'm sure you can show yourselves out."

Taking Caden by the hand, he headed to the foyer.

"Wait!" His mother came after him and tried to grab his arm.

He pulled away from her reach. "What?"

She licked her lower lip with an expression of uncertainty that he'd never seen before. "We need to talk this out. We need to find a solution. You're our only heir, Tate."

"Yeah, it's a bummer, huh? You should have popped out more spares, Mom."

"There's no need for you to be vulgar."

"There's no need for you to be a bitch, either, but here we are. Let's go," he said to Caden.

"No!" His mother reached for him again as his father came to join her. "Tell us what you want."

Oh, how those words cost her. For the first time in his life, he saw vulnerability in his parents. If not for how they had treated, and continued to treat, Caden, he might have felt sympathy, and hope that they could forge a better relationship. That time had passed, however. He felt liberated and in control of his life for the first time without having to be risking death to do so.

"I'll give it some thought." He went to the closet and helped Caden into his jacket before donning his own. "You can start by emancipating all of your debt slaves without penalty."

He could tell by their expressions that they didn't like that. But they weren't fools.

His mother nodded. "All right."

"And don't buy any replacements. Hire employees for a fair wage."

"Fine," his father bit out. "What else?"

"I'll let you know." He opened the door and ushered Caden outside. Then he shut it right on his parents' fuming faces.

It was a beautiful sunny day with spring in the air. He took Caden's hand and walked him down the front stoop and turned right to walk to Newbury Street. He needed to get in touch with his lawyer to put his papers in order and start his new life. That chore could wait, however. He'd found his wallet waiting for him at home and had been smart enough to keep his finances separate and safe from his parents. He was his own man, and for now, he would enjoy a day with the beautiful boy he loved.

Caden pressed against his side. "You handled them very well, darling. I'm sorry they made it so difficult."

He squeezed his hand. "You're the one they insulted. I won't tolerate it, but I'm also not going to tell them that accepting you is one of the things they have to do if they want a relationship with me. Some things they have to figure out on their own because it's the right thing to do, not out of cold calculation."

Caden chuckled. "I think you're expecting too much now. And I really don't care what they think of me."

Tate stopped and pulled Caden in close by his waist. "You should. I do because you are the most wonderful person in the world. Loving you means everything to me. Your loving me back is like a little miracle."

Caden cupped Tate's face. "It hasn't been easy, I must confess. You were high-handed and a pain in the ass when I first met you, after all." He grinned, ruining the teasing.

Tate laughed and hugged Caden tight. "God, I love you. Let's get married today. I can fly us to Vegas and…" He stopped talking when Caden smacked him on the ass.

"No. No quickie marriage by Elvis. But I'll let you buy me a ring after breakfast."

"Oh, now that does sound like fun." He started them walking again. "I wouldn't have thought I'd ever say this but smacking face-first into a tree was the best thing to happen to me."

"Given how it turned out, I have to agree." Now it was Caden who stopped. He looked earnestly into Tate's eyes. "You know that I don't care about your money, right? I'd take you with only the clothes on your back, the same way you're taking me. You are my love, my future…and my master, no matter what."

"I know." He kissed him because it was impossible not to. "Let's go eat, shop, then return home and play master and slave. If you're a good boy, I'll let you ride me again."

"If you're a good master, I'll let you do whatever you want. There won't be a pineapple to be heard."

Grinning at each other like fools, they headed into their future.

Sign up for our newsletter and find out about all our romance book releases, eBook sales and promotions, sneak peeks and FREE romance books!

Want to see more from this author? Here's a taster for you to enjoy!

Debt Slave: His Undercover Slave
Samantha Cayto

Excerpt

Special Agent Cole Cooper stared at the bloody, mangled bodies of teenagers strewn over the concrete floor of the warehouse. *What a fucking waste.* Most of these boys had been headed for long stretches in the maximum-security facility in Menard, and a few were never going to make it to their thirties anyway. Still, the sight of the effect of having so much firepower at their fingertips when the turf war had gone down was stomach-churning.

The sound of his boss' light tread had him briefly closing his eyes. "I should have found out about this sooner."

"You're not a rookie anymore, Cooper. You ought to know by now that you can't save everyone, and you can't stop every bad thing that's going to happen. As it is, you got us here fast enough to round up a couple of dozen gang members and keep about a million dollars' worth of heroin off the street. From where I'm standing, that's a good night's work."

He turned away from the carnage to stare at the Special Agent in Charge's concerned face. The woman had grown up on the South Side of Chicago and what she hadn't seen in her childhood, she'd most certainly experienced in her twenty years as an FBI agent. She was right, of course. Still…

"If they hadn't had these weapons, the fallout would have been less." He tugged at the mop of too-long hair he'd grown for his undercover work. "I know I'm preaching to the choir, ma'am, but we've got to find a way to choke off at least this one source of illegal arms."

His boss grimaced and, patting him on the shoulder, deftly steered him out of the building and into the cool night air. Spring in Chicago held a nip in the air. He hunched into his ratty jacket as he took in the scene of federal agents, local police and morgue personnel working to clean up the aftermath of the firefight.

His boss waited until they'd closed in on her car before speaking again.

"Go home, take a few days off. This has been a long assignment and you've had pretty much non-stop ones since coming out of Quantico. You need the down time."

Cole knew she was right. He'd been undercover in multiple places in the year since he'd earned his badge. He'd barely seen his family during that time. But there was a reason for the using him so much. The boyish face that made him a believable teenager in high schools wasn't going to last much longer. Already, he could see a maturity—a hardness—setting in around his eyes. He was never going to get taller and was probably going to keep his slender frame, if his father was any indication of his future self. His face, though, wasn't going to hold its youthful appearance forever. Once it was gone, his usefulness in this kind of street-level undercover work was going to end. He had to make the most of it while it lasted.

The boss gestured toward the agent who drove her around. "Andre, take Cole home. His real one," she added unnecessarily, because this assignment was over.

"Thank you, ma'am. He doesn't have to do that. I can take the L."

She gave him the side-eye. "Did I ask you?"

Cole grimaced. "No, ma'am."

"Then get in the damn car."

The woman shot him a look of irritation before turning back to oversee the clean-up of the worst gangland war the city had seen in years.

Cole dutifully rounded the car and slid into the passenger seat. With his ass down, the weariness that had threatened to overtake him gained traction. He closed his eyes and laid his head back as he fumbled blindly to fasten his seatbelt.

"Tough night," Andre commented as he started up the car. "I'm sure you feel like shit right now, but you did good, dude."

"Eight guys cut to ribbons. Christ, Sean Finch's head was blown off." Because the image of the carnage rose vividly in his mind, he popped his eyes open to stare at the city lights.

"Yeah well, that's what happens with assault weapons. Every one of those dead boys knew what they were getting into. Or should have, anyway. That's a lot of firepower to play with."

"I know." Cole rubbed his forehead. It was throbbing from tension and lack of sleep. "And handgun or a switchblade can make you just as dead." He pounded his thigh with a clenched fist. "If I'd had more time, I could have found out the name of their arms dealer. Maybe we could have intercepted the shipment."

Andre tsked as he shook his head. "That was secondary to the assignment. The drugs were paramount and you did your job there. Not your fault that a rival gang had decided to horn in on this territory."

"Right." He understood all of this and still couldn't shake his sense of failure. "If we could only stop the main source of the guns coming into this city, that would go a long way to keeping everyone a little safer."

"Above our pay-grade, dude." Andre pulled over to the curb.

It took a moment for Cole's exhausted brain to recognize his own building. No real surprise there. He spent very little time living in his apartment.

He unbuckled himself and opened his door. "Thanks, man."

"Any time."

Andre waited until Cole keyed into the lobby before taking off. As if he was bringing a date safely home, or something. Not that any of Cole's dates ever ended up simply dropping him off. He was pretty basic when it came to sex. If he went out with a guy, it was because he wanted to fuck him. If it turned into something more, great. The idea of marriage and even kids was something he believed in. It wasn't in the cards for him just yet. It might never be, he knew. There weren't many happily married FBI agents in his acquaintance. Divorce was rampant because the demands of the job put a hell of a lot of stress on a relationship. Getting laid once in a while was the best he could hope for at this point in his career.

He took the elevator to the second floor, testament to how worn out he truly was. When he entered his apartment, it was almost like being in a foreign land. The place was so still, as if nothing lived there. A coat of dust testified to his absence. He kicked off the designer high-tops his undercover role had demanded and continued to shed every article of clothing he'd been given specifically for this job. By the time he entered his bedroom, he was down to his skin. For the first time in weeks, he felt like himself. There was enough light coming in from the street, that he didn't bother turning on any lamps.

As much as he wanted sleep, he wanted to wash the grime of his assignment off first. He turned the temperature of the shower to as hot as he could stand it, and stood braced against the tiled wall and let the water cascade over him. Fear of falling asleep right where he was had him forcing his body to move. He washed his too long hair and scrubbed his skin until it screamed at him to stop. When he stepped out of the shower, he wiped the fog from the mirror over the sink and stared long and hard at the image. Naked and wet or dry and clothed, he still looked like a kid—a very pretty one. It made him very good at his job and it easy to pick up men. No one took him seriously. A party boy. A twink. God, he hated that term, yet here he was, exploiting his image. Sometimes for the greater good, and others as a way to not be lonely for a few hours.

"Now you're just being maudlin," he told his image.

Swiping the towel across his skin and hair, he went to his dresser. He pulled out a pair of boxer briefs and an old T-shirt. Settling down under the covers, he closed his eyes. But as soon as he did, visions of blood and gore and wasted lives flooded in. His whole body tensed and the effects of his shower evaporated faster than the water droplets had. With a muted cry of frustration, he sat up, rubbing his face. Then he yanked open the nightstand drawer and pulled out his laptop.

He didn't have any official files on it, naturally. But he'd done research of his own, the kind the internet allowed anyone to access. He opened the file labelled *Volpe* and stared at a face he knew almost as well as his own. Enzo Volpe. The asshole had become the largest arms dealer in the world. Based on a yacht, the guy moved around a lot, never within the jurisdiction of any one country for very long. No one knew where he'd come from. His name implied he was Italian and his dark, almost sultry, good looks implied he was. But no one had been able to trace him back to his origins. And his fluency in the language meant nothing. He was equally skilled in five other languages, including English. The man could have been raised right here in Chicago for all his accent betrayed.

All Cole, or anyone, really knew was that countless people around the world were dead because of this man's immoral trade. The gang members in the warehouse were merely the most recent that he knew of. Dozens, hundreds probably, more were dying as Cole lay there in his cozy little apartment. That was the problem with Volpe. He caused death around the clock, no matter where he was or what he was doing. *Probably lapping champagne off some model's abs.* The man was a hedonist and his dirty money could pay for a lot of it. Other than well-paid goons and servants, no one got close to him. A few global agencies had tried and everyone they'd sent in undercover had disappeared. When you lived on a boat, disposing of enemies was easy.

Because dwelling on the arms dealer made him sicker to his stomach than he already was, Cole forced himself to shut the laptop down and settle back into his pillow. Then he went through the relaxation techniques that a Quantico buddy had taught him and slipped into oblivion.

* * * *

"So, you're kicking me to the curb."

Roman Noone stared out at Boston Harbor, admiring the way the setting sun still glistened off the water, and trying to suppress a sigh. "Don't be so dramatic, Joanathan. I don't have the time to vacation in Cape Town and don't particularly want to."

Been there. Done that.

"But we had so much fun there the last time, baby. And I have a few weeks before my next film starts shooting. I need to do some serious relaxing."

Roman flopped down into his desk chair, flipping through the memories of what downtime looked like to the movie star. Sure, there was lots of lazy swimming in a pool and energetic sex on silk sheets. But there was also endless paparazzi when they went out. It *had* been fun for a while. Roman liked the attention, for the most part, and Jonathan loved showing off his "billionaire boyfriend", as the press had dubbed him. Like everything else, however, it had become boring. Meaningless. And a chore to boot. That restless feeling had built inside him, as it always did, causing him to look for life elsewhere.

"I have work. You know that."

"Yeah, and I know you can do that from South Africa as well you can in your ivory tower at One Financial Center." Jonathan blew noisily into the phone, a sign he was vaping more than being frustrated.

"And you can find any number of entertaining men in Cape Town. Unless you want to spend your time with me here in Boston." He knew the invitation would be turned down. An A-list actor wasn't going to molder in Roman's home in Louisburg Square.

"Fuck you, Roman. You're not that great a lay."

The connection went dead. Roman put his own phone down without a twinge of guilt. The relationship with Jonathan had always been light and frankly transactional. There was no love there, on either of their parts, or even a particular affection. And his bitchy now-ex-lover had been lying about that last part. Roman happened to know he was excellent in bed. Jonathan had cultivated a tough-guy image in the movies, which perversely was enhanced by his being openly gay. When it came to sex, however, the man loved to be dominated. Roman had been more than happy to oblige him and could be counted on to keep his mouth shut about it.

Well, there was no sense in dwelling on this most recent not-so-gentle uncoupling. There was work to be done. There always was, no matter the time or day, something he relished because he worked for himself.

The door to his office opened with two sharp raps.

"Knock, knock." His executive assistant always knocked and vocalized his doing so even as he opened the door without waiting for an invitation.

Roman had found the habit annoying at first, as he had the boy's flirty nature. His stellar skills as an admin, and his obvious fidelity to his husband, had quickly won him over. Oliver might appear to be an empty-headed twink, but he had the mind of a computer, the organization of a platoon sergeant, and the loyalty of a hound dog.

"What's up, Oliver?"

The boy shut the door and sauntered over to the desk with a conspiratorial expression. "The FBI is here to see you. What have you been up to, boss?"

Roman raised his eyebrows. "You mean the Federal Bureau of Investigation?"

Oliver cocked his hip. "Do you know of another organization with those initials?"

Roman couldn't resist teasing. "I don't know. It could be the newest boy band you're into."

"None of my celebrity hall passes carry guns."

Roman rose to his feet with a narrowed gaze. "They've come in armed?"

Oliver shrugged. "Unless their armpits are just happy to see me."

"Did they say what they wanted?" He flicked his gaze to the ormolu clock on his desk. "It's after eight." Not that he kept anything like 'normal' officer hours but it did strike him as strange that government employees would show up at this hour unless it was an emergency.

"I did point out the lateness of their visit, to which they indicated that was the point."

Very strange. And just a bit interesting. Roman wasn't concerned. He was a straight-arrow when it came to running both his businesses and his personal life. "And refused to say why they're here?"

"For your ears only, boss. And your evening is free, so…"

"Send them in. But don't offer them coffee. I don't like the arrogance of assuming I'd see them at this hour, or any hour, for that matter."

"Too late," Oliver said over his shoulder. "Already offered and rejected."

Seconds later, his admin ushered in two people. One was an African American woman a little older then himself, he judged. She was tall and fierce-looking. He had no trouble believing she was FBI. The other agent had him doing a double take. The man—no, boy—was hardly anyone's idea of a law-enforcement officer. Not quite even average height and slender, he looked like he was still in high school. And wasn't merely adorable the way Oliver was. This kid was drop-dead gorgeous. His longish, shaggy hair was a true black and his eyes a bright blue. The pale skin of his face and his delicate features brought out both protective instincts and an instant hard-on.

He forced himself to focus on the woman.

She marched right up to his desk and held out her hand. "Mr. Noone, I'm Special Agent in Charge Rhonda Johnson out of Chicago."

He shook, then pulled back his own hand as she turned to introduce her colleague, not wanting even such casual contact with the too-appealing boy.

"This is Special Agent Cole Cooper."

The young man didn't seem any more interested in a handshake than Roman did. He stayed farther away, standing stiffly in his ill-fitting suit.

"Sir."

Roman gestured toward his visitor chairs. "Please have a seat and tell me why you've chosen to simply show up at my office this late."

Johnson grimaced as she sat. "I'm sorry, sir. What we have to discuss with you requires as much secrecy as we can accomplish. Prior communication was deemed too risky and we wanted to time our arrival when your offices were as empty as possible."

Roman raised his eyebrows, intrigued despite his irritation. If nothing else, the next few minutes might prove diverting. "Indeed? Well, best get right to it, then."

Johnson took a moment before speaking. "Have you ever heard of Enzo Volpe?"

Roman searched his memory. "Perhaps."

"He's an arms dealer."

"Interesting. And you think I might know him because...I run in the same circles?" The idea was laughable. He couldn't stop the grin.

"No, actually, sir, we're speaking to you because we know you don't. Your businesses are all legitimate."

"If not always moral," the boy, Cooper, added in a low voice.

Johnson shot her companion a quelling look, but as he was staring at Roman and not her, he missed it.

Amused now as well as intrigued, Roman turned his attention to the boy. "You don't approve of my version of capitalism, Agent Cooper?"

Cooper flicked him a look that was designed to make a man's balls tighten with desire. Or at least, that was Roman's reaction. Before the question got answered, Johnson jumped in again.

"We are here because we need your help, Mr. Noone."

Roman stared at Cooper until the boy lowered his gaze. "Help how?" he asked, his focus back on the woman.

"The United States, as well as other countries, have been trying to bring Volpe down for years. He's managed to evade arrest and keeps the records that could put him out of business and in jail on his yacht. As far as we can tell. No one can get close to him and those that have tried are missing and presumed dead."

"I can well imagine. Ruthlessness fits my vision of what an arms dealer would be like. I still don't understand what you want from me. Borrow my yacht? I don't use it much, mostly for business and social gatherings, and being out to sea doesn't interest me as much as it does other people."

"No, sir. Transportation isn't the issue. Gaining Volpe's trust is." Johnson shifted, tugging at her suitcoat. "We've been working with Interpol on how to get someone else inside, gain Volpe's confidence, get on that yacht of his."

Roman leaned back in his chair, very interested now in what the FBI was cooking up. "You think I have a way in?"

"No, but we believe you can play the part we need to gain access."

"And end up fish bait, too?"

Johnson looked him square in the eye. "There is that chance, yes. The thing is," she continued before he could respond to that stark truth, "you can get in because you are clearly not with law enforcement. Everyone knows Roman Noone. You'd pass any background check he might do with the truth of your life. Volpe will accept you for what you are and won't suspect you're a plant."

The boy agent picked up the conversational ball. "Volpe likes socializing with the legitimately rich and famous. He doesn't keep a low profile, which allows easier contact with him to be made. And he's openly gay."

Roman blinked in surprise at that tidbit. "That's surprising. I wouldn't expect his usual customers to be progressive thinkers."

"Nobody fucks with Volpe. His being out is testament to how dangerous he really is."

"And yet, you want me to beard the lion in his den?"

"We don't expect you to do anything more than gain his confidence. Get an invitation to join him on his yacht. He often socializes on it for days at a time. The fact that you also don't have a security team trailing you everywhere you go will put Volpe at ease."

"I don't need babysitters. I can take care of myself." It was a point of pride that he'd gone through the necessary training to protect himself.

"Exactly. Not that he'll see it that way. He'll assume you are easily contained, if need be. The only armed people there will be his, which hopefully will make him let down his guard."

Cooper chimed in. "Naturally, we'll protect you to the best of our ability. You should be safe." He looked at Roman with a straight face, as if he truly believed what he said.

"Hopefully. I expect my predecessors thought the same thing." Roman made it sound like he was more concerned than he was. Maybe he was an idiot and maybe he'd become too bored with life, but he wasn't laughing these people out of his office. Not yet. Even though he obviously should.

Johnson retook control of the conversation. "Yes, hopefully. We can't tell you this isn't dangerous."

"And unorthodox, I imagine. I'm sure you turn inside people all the time to work for you in exchange for leniency."

"Volpe makes sure everyone who works for him is more afraid of what he'll do than any law enforcement. No one close to Volpe is approachable."

"But I am?" Roman let his amusement show. "You've got nothing to hold over me."

"Just your sense of patriotism." This from Cooper.

Roman turned his gaze to the boy again. He let a little of the heat he was feeling into his eyes. Enough to see the boy squirm slightly.

"I say the pledge of allegiance at every game I attend for my baseball team and give generously to organizations that help first responders. No one has ever called me unpatriotic."

"Nor are we," Johnson was quick to interject. "We, frankly, are at wit's end about how to stop Volpe."

"And if you succeed, won't there be others to take his place? I imagine it's like trying to empty the ocean one cup at a time."

"You're right. Stopping Volpe won't end arms dealing. It will make a good dent, however, and it will take years for someone else to build up the empire he has. We need his files, Mr. Noone. That information will allow us to take out his entire operation."

Roman considered what he was being asked to do. It was on the face of it, insane. "I loved James Bond as a kid but I can't quite see myself skulking around Volpe's yacht, cracking into his computer and jet skiing myself to safety. I'm tough and have pretty steady nerves. Life isn't a movie, though. You need a professional."

Perhaps sensing victory, Johnson leaned forward. "We'll have one. With you. No one expects you to do anything other than use your famous name to gain Volpe's friendship. As Agent Cooper said, he likes surrounding himself with legitimate jet-setters and you are one of the most visible ones who isn't a celebrity with paparazzi always dogging his heels. You get just enough press to be known and interesting without being under constant scrutiny. Volpe won't be able to resist cultivating your acquaintance and even might feel you out about joining his network. You have a lot of merchant ships moving goods around the globe."

Roman held up his hand. "Wait. You just said that every other undercover agent has been compromised. How do you expect to get one in with me?"

"We've going to give you a debt slave. It's the perfect cover. A debt slave will have your name and travel on your passport. There will be nothing for anyone to check up on. No one pays attention to them anyway. And even those countries that haven't adopted the practice honor the status of US citizens as such."

"What?" Roman wanted to laugh. "You're going to have an agent pose as a debt slave that I own? I find that whole system distasteful. Everyone who works for me is an employee. That's an easy matter to learn. Why would I suddenly acquire one?"

Now Johnson looked uncomfortable. "You have a reputation of picking up men and discarding them relatively quickly. Trading in boyfriends for a no-strings personal slave makes perfect sense."

Roman wasn't often stunned into silence. This was one of those times. He was offended by the concept the FBI's plan was based on, yet also couldn't deny that there was both truth and logic to it.

"That was one of the most repugnant things anyone has ever said to me, although you're not wrong. Sadly."

"We'll be pairing you with a seasoned agent with undercover experience who can also play his part to perfection. He'll protect you, as well. The fact that he won't seem like he could is one of the things this plan hitches on."

Clarity came suddenly and he felt stupid that he hadn't instantly copped to what the woman had in mind. Planting his elbows on his desk, he leaned toward Cooper. "You."

The boy nodded. "Me."

About the Author

Samantha Cayto is a Boston-area native who practices as a business lawyer by day while writing erotic romance at night—the steamier the better. She likes to push the envelope when it comes to writing about passion and is delighted other women agree that guy-on-guy sex is the hottest ever.

She lives a typical suburban life with her husband, three kids and four dogs. Her children don't understand why they can't read what she writes, but her husband is always willing to lend her a hand—and anything else—when she needs to choreograph a scene.

Samantha loves to hear from readers. You can find her contact information, website details and author profile page at https://www.firstforromance.com

ENTWINED PUBLISHING

www.ingramcontent.com/pod-product-compliance
Lightning Source LLC
Chambersburg PA
CBHW050532260626
47157CB00004B/1564